WHISPERS THROUGH TIME

Melanie Robertson-King

King Park Press

Published by King Park Press

Copyright © Melanie Robertson-King,
2024
House image:Arianna Tavaglione
(Pexels)
Poem Antigonish by William Hughes
Mearns (Public Domain)

WHISPERS THROUGH TIME is a work of fiction.
Names, characters, places and incidents are the
product of the author's imagination or are used
fictitiously. Any resemblance to actual events,
locales or persons, living or dead, is purely
coincidental.

ISBN: 978-1-990371-08-0

DEDICATION

For those who have experienced whispers through time.

ACKNOWLEDGMENTS

Thanks to Joanna Penn and Joseph Michael for their informative workshop on ChatGPT. It turned out to be a great brainstorming partner.

Huge thanks to my eagle-eyed proof/beta reader Nancy Chapman.

If I've missed anyone by name, I apologize.

Special thanks to my husband, Don, who continues to support and encourage me, and provides a shoulder to cry on when things don't go well. He redesigned my website making it mobile-friendly and taken charge on the domestic front giving me time to write.

Chapter One

Albert Kembleford stormed into his study, turned the key in the lock and left it in the door. When he crossed the room to his desk, the letter from the bank that had arrived in the mail earlier in the day taunted him. The body was bad enough, but did the institution have to humiliate him further with the word FORECLOSURE stamped in red on the white space near the top of the letterhead?

He knew it would come to this. A year ago, he began funnelling money from his lumberyard into his personal accounts to maintain the mortgage payments on their home and lavish lifestyle. Six months later, the money ran out. Albert never told his wife they were in financial trouble. It wasn't done. Being the breadwinner and provider for his family fell on his shoulders. He couldn't bear his family knowing he was a failure.

The time had come. Albert reached into the middle left drawer of his desk, pulled out his Smith and Wesson revolver, and ensured the chamber was fully loaded. He had one chance to do it and wanted nothing left to error.

His crystal decanter of single malt stood on a tray with matching glasses. He'd have one before his time on this earth was up. Dutch courage. One for the road. He poured three fingers into the tumbler — two wouldn't be enough. A ray of sun beaming through in the window glinted off the cuts in the glass, making it sparkle,

1

illuminating the amber liquid so that it glowed.

He would miss this house and the town of Pike Falls, where he had chosen to settle and make his fortune. Too bad it didn't turn out that way. He gulped down the whisky and returned the glass to its proper place. Only then did he sit behind his desk. The same place where he completed paperwork for his lumber empire — ha! — many times.

As much as he wanted to burn the letter, he couldn't. He needed to leave it for his wife Patience to find so she wouldn't feel guilty, thinking it was something she did to make him do what he was about to. Across the bottom of the letter, he scrawled *I'm sorry, dearest Patience. Please forgive me. Love always, Albert.*

Then he cocked the gun, placed the end of the barrel against his temple, and pulled the trigger.

Chapter Two

OCTOBER 14, 2022

Nicole Holbrook pulled her compact Chevy into a parking bay in front of the business she and her older twin brothers operated, CNC IT Solutions, in a strip mall on the outskirts of town. The back seat and hatch were filled with boxes. Usually, she parked her car behind the building, but with all the family documents and who knew what else the cartons contained, she wanted to leave her car where she could keep an eye on it from her desk. She grabbed her computer bag and cell phone and dashed into the office, using the remote on the key fob to lock her vehicle as she went.

"You're late," said Cooper.

"Dad phoned me and asked me to meet him at the storage locker. He was clearing out the last of Mummy's things and wanted us to have them."

"Did you forget we have that Zoom meeting with the Barnsleys this morning?"

"I'm here now, so what's your problem." Her brother continued to scowl at her. "Oh, and you can quit with the stink eye anytime."

Her other brother, Connor, appeared from the kitchenette, holding a steaming coffee mug. "Hey, sis. Coop giving you a hard time again?"

"Nothing I can't handle." She walked past Cooper's chair and swatted the back of his head on her way to her desk.

"You got those sketches ready for the meeting?"

"Yes." Nicole pulled her sketchbook out of her computer bag, along with a pencil case. It was old-fashioned designing logos with coloured pencils and paper rather than directly on the computer, but it was a method that worked best for her. Once the designs were tweaked and finally approved, she scanned her drawing and, using photo editing software, created layers to make the digital version.

Artwork of Nicole's creation adorned the walls, intermingled with their diplomas and other certificates of achievement.

"I've got half a dozen preliminary sketches done. Hopefully, they'll like what I've come up with." She opened her sketchbook to the first page of drawings.

Cooper initiated the Zoom meeting, and they gathered in front of the large monitor connected to his computer. During first-time online conferences, the three siblings stayed at their own workstations, but they used just one when Nicole's designs were on show.

As their discussions continued, Nicole tweaked the favourite of the designs. At the end of the meeting, the approval had been received for the new logo for Barnsley's Bakery. Now, she could get the sketch into the computer and finish the work.

"You guys up for a little urban exploration tomorrow?" Connor asked.

"What did you have in mind?" Cooper responded.

"How about this place?" Connor turned his monitor around so his siblings could see the picture on his screen.

"Kembleford Manor. The once stately home of lumber baron, Albert Kembleford and his family, was converted to a hotel in the 1940s after the war. It didn't stay open for long. The hoteliers gave it up after several unexplained events scared guests away," Cooper read aloud.

"Ghosts, maybe?" Nicole suggested.

"Could be. Where is this place?"

"Pike Falls. It's about a six-hour drive each way, so we'd have to get away early in the morning," said

Connor. "I've Google mapped it on this tab." He switched tabs in the browser and brought up the map and the suggested route.

"I'm game," said Cooper.

"Kembleford. Kembleford. Where have I heard that name before? Or did I see it somewhere?" Nicole mused.

"Duh, the village in *Father Brown*. You watch it all the time," said Connor.

"No. Not that. I know it from something else. Why can't I remember?"

Connor was pleased his suggested location had been agreed upon. Usually, the places they ventured to were all Cooper's ideas, and he and his sister acquiesced to them.

The rest of the day passed quickly for Connor, working alongside his brother to design the website to the client's specifications. His sister's desk butted against his, and after she'd scanned the new logo for the site, she worked quietly. The office's only sounds were the tapping of computer keys and the click of mouse buttons. Occasionally, the clack of her bracelets against her keyboard disrupted the relative silence.

Nicole watched the clock as she wondered what was in the boxes her father gave her at the storage locker. All her mother's clothes had been donated to charity in the weeks following her death, so it wasn't anything like that. Her dad hadn't been forthcoming about the contents; he just said it was things that belonged to his late wife and that since he was giving up the rented space, anything she or her brothers didn't take was going to the dump.

Since her mother had died, her father rarely spoke of her. He acted as though the woman never existed. She supposed it was his way of grieving. Nicole kicked herself for never asking about her maternal grandparents when she was younger. She barely remembered her grandfather. He died of a massive heart attack when she was three. Her grandmother had dementia in her later years and died not knowing any members of her family, but her memory was sharp as a tack for events twenty or more years prior.

Not being able to go through the things tortured her. And now, with going on a long drive to check out an old abandoned mansion the next day, she wouldn't have the opportunity to even look through everything she'd piled into her small car. The hatch was packed, not that it was a huge space; the backseat and even the front passenger seat had boxes piled on it. Maybe she should have left her car in the lot behind the strip mall. At least if it was out back, she wouldn't see it and be constantly reminded of the mystery of what those cardboard cartons contained.

And what about the name Kembleford? She knew it from the television show, but she had heard the name before. Did her mother say something? Her father? Or was it one of those memories her grandmother could recall with accuracy?

She turned her attention back to the design on her computer screen. When the client approved her artwork, she was excited and couldn't wait to get it digitized. Now it looked flat and lifeless. It lacked something. The Barnsley's Bakery logo was as deflated as a bowl of yeast dough punched down after rising. She picked up her sketchbook and flipped through the pages to the approved hand-rendered version. The image on her screen looked nothing like what she had drawn. The only thing the two had in common was the shape.

Nicole removed her glasses, dropped them on her desk, and ran her fingers through her long hair. She pressed her palms against the sides of her head. "Argh," she grunted.

"Not going well?" Connor asked.

"No." She stood and walked away from her desk. "Why is it not working? How come it looks great on paper and like something a kid would draw on the computer?"

"Take a break, sis," said Cooper. "Grab a coffee. Maybe when you come back and look at it again, you'll see what you need to do to fix it."

"I don't think that will do any good, but I could

use a coffee." She walked to the back of the office, where the kitchenette was located, and popped a pod into their coffee machine. It had taken some convincing to get Cooper to go along with this purchase; he thought the drip coffeemaker was good enough. That was because he was never lumbered with making a pot. Or getting the skanky dregs after it had sat too long. Now, every cup was fresh, and they each made their own — even had their preferred blends.

When the workday ended, Nicole was no closer to coming to a solution for the graphic. Maybe after getting away from it for the entire weekend, she'd see the problem clearly on Monday.

"Bye, guys. See you in the morning," she called out as she dashed out the front door to her car.

Her sketchbook remained on her desk. It was the one she used for work. The others, her personal ones, waited at her apartment. Her apartment. Up three flights of stairs. The building didn't have an elevator. She would have to carry the boxes from her car up one at a time and then return for the next. The only good thing about that was she could get credit for doing loads of stairs. Zone minutes, too.

Chapter Three

OCTOBER 15, 2022

Nicole was ready for their adventure early Saturday morning. She wore neutral-coloured clothes and a pair of beige canvas running shoes on her feet. From the pictures on Connor's computer screen, it was difficult to gauge the isolation surrounding the abandoned hotel. Hopefully, it was well off the beaten track so they wouldn't be interrupted or, worse still, have the police show up and escort them off the property. The latter had happened on previous occasions, but luckily, they hadn't gained access to the buildings themselves, so they were let off with warnings.

The night before, she charged the battery in her camera, formatted a new SD card, and put fresh batteries in the external flash unit. The built-in flash was sometimes sufficient, but occasionally, if the windows were boarded up, the other worked better.

A car horn sounded, and Nicole looked out the window. Cooper's SUV was parked on the street across from her apartment. She scooped up her khaki coloured backpack containing her camera equipment, sketchbook, pencils (she never went anywhere without them), and her apartment key and dashed out the door and down to the street.

Connor occupied the front passenger seat. She couldn't remember when she got to ride shotgun on one of their sojourns. Shoving her gear into the back, she clambered into the vehicle and settled in the middle so she could look out the windshield rather than at a headrest all the way to Pike Falls.

The early morning sun on the autumn leaves accentuated their brilliant shades of red, yellow, orange, and brown. Once out of the city, Nicole grabbed her sketchbook and a pencil and began sketching the bucolic countryside they passed through.

For most of the trip, the weather was clear and calm, but the closer they got to Pike Falls, the darker it became. The rain pelted down, at first in random drops splatting against the windshield, before becoming torrential. Even with the wipers on full speed, they couldn't keep up with the downpour. The wind picked up and tore the coloured leaves from the trees. Gunmetal grey clouds scudded across the sky. Treetops swayed violently.

"It's almost like Kembleford Manor is telling us to stay away," said Nicole.

"Do ya think?" asked Cooper. "If our expedition goes pear-shaped, we can blame it on Connor. It was his idea we come here."

"Like I can control the weather."

Those words were no sooner out of his mouth, when lightning streaked across the sky, followed closely by a booming clap of thunder.

"That was close," said Nicole. "I don't mind storms, but this is too close for comfort."

Another flash and a tree along the side of the road burst into flames, and a large branch toppled down. Cooper slammed on the brakes and managed to stop the vehicle before they hit the downed limb. The sudden braking threw Nicole forward, but the shoulder strap of her seatbelt locked, preventing her from being tossed into the front seat or maybe even the windshield.

"Everybody okay?" Cooper asked.

"Isn't it a bit too late in the year for thunderstorms?" asked Connor.

"I still think it's Kembleford Manor sending us a message," said Nicole.

"In 300 yards, turn right," the computerized voice of the GPS said.

"That's all well and good, but it's impossible with

a chunk of tree blocking the road."

"Can we move it? Or is it too heavy?" Nicole asked.

"We can try," Cooper said.

The siblings piled out of the vehicle and moved towards the fallen limb. Cooper and Connor grabbed onto smaller branches and tugged. It moved, but not much. Nicole climbed over, and she pushed the next time her brothers pulled. It took a long time, but eventually, they managed to move it from across the road.

Back in the SUV, Cooper put the vehicle in gear and they carried on with their journey.

Then, in decreasing 100-yard increments, the device spoke again.

After Cooper made the turn, the storm abated. Was it just a coincidence that they were going to an abandoned house when the foul weather hit? Or was it something more sinister?

The GPS spoke again, indicating a left turn ahead.

Cooper turned onto a narrow gravel road. That was too kind a description for it. Two rows of tire tracks were separated by a strip of grass. Potholes lined the road. He dropped the SUV into second gear and eased it along the path.

"You have reached your destination."

There was no house. Nothing to indicate it had ever stood in the immediate area.

"Hey, isn't that Mitch's truck up ahead?" asked Cooper.

"Why would he be here? There must be a lot of trucks in the province that are that make and colour," Nicole answered.

Cooper eased the SUV up behind the truck. As he did, Mitchell climbed out.

"Okay, which one of you two told him we were coming here today?"

"I sure as hell didn't," said Connor.

"Neither did I," replied Nicole.

Mitchell Kane was a rival urban explorer, and

they had never collaborated on sites. Cooper climbed from the SUV and strode towards the man through the fallen, wet leaves. The earthy smell reached his nostrils but did nothing for his mood. Had his competitor not been standing in front of him with his arms folded across his chest, the soothing aroma might have had some effect.

"Who invited you?" Cooper demanded.

"No one."

"It seems too much of a coincidence that you're here on the same day we came to check out the place."

"Maybe you three got the idea from me," Mitch countered before his expression softened.

Cooper caught sight of Nicole on his left through his peripheral vision. The change in his adversary's stance was apparent to him now. The guy was sweet on his sister. It had to be her fault that he was here. He'd deal with Nicole later, but his primary focus was on the man standing before him.

"Are we going to stand out here in the rain debating who told whom, or are we going inside?" asked Nicole as she ran her hands through her hair to remove the excess moisture.

Her brothers returned to the SUV and unpacked the gear they brought along to explore the abandoned hotel. She opened the rear passenger door, pulled out her backpack, and slung it over her shoulder.

Cooper and Connor led the way up the gravel track, continuing in the direction they'd driven. She walked a few paces behind them with Mitch. At least Cooper had stopped posturing, but how long that would last remained unknown. She was a big girl and could look after herself without his intervention, although sometimes his gesture was appreciated. But Mitch? He was practically a brother. The three boys were constantly together when they were younger — the three Musketeers. Nicole was the odd person out once she was old enough to tag along. Even when her brothers first started exploring abandoned houses and other structures, she wasn't invited to accompany them. Too dangerous for a girl, they said. There were other excuses, too, but the danger one stuck with her.

"Mitch, how'd you find this place?" she asked. "It's too much of a coincidence that you showed up here the same day we did.

He turned and smiled. "I could tell you, but then I'd have to kill you." He chuckled.

She wasn't going to get any information from him. At least not yet.

The vicious storm they drove through to get here finally tapered off, but the sun remained behind the thick cloud layer. Nicole shrugged her backpack off her shoulder and pulled out her camera, putting the strap over her head.

Ahead, her brothers stopped. A chain with a KEEP OUT sign dangling from it at about the midpoint stretched across the track. At least the barrier was low enough that they could step over it. Even from this vantage point, the house remained hidden. Shrubs that hadn't been maintained for years blocked the sight of anything manmade.

Finally, the lane widened and a chipped and faded sign announcing the Kembleford Manor Hotel greeted them. Beyond it stood the granite double-fronted mansion with bay windows on both the ground and second floors. A tower nestled between them. Both it and the house had mansard roofs. The topmost window in the building was a dormer with a rounded top. Where was the entrance? Nicole brought her camera up and began snapping pictures of the front façade.

Weeds had taken over the gravel driveway and the centre of what appeared to be a roundabout. Off to one side, the gravel continued straight. Was that the direction of the front door? Maybe what Nicole assumed was the front was actually one side.

Cooper's temper simmered on a low boil. How dare Mitchell Kane insert himself into his and his siblings' day? The first chance he got, he'd question his sister. He wasn't blind. He saw the way Nicole and Mitch looked at one another. And Mitch's change in stance once he saw her.

For now, he had more important things to consider. Firstly, how to gain entry. The door was locked. One thing he never carried with him was lock picking tools. That was a sure way to get arrested for a far more serious crime than just trespass. This old place was far enough off the beaten path that a police patrol shouldn't be a problem.

He checked the windows, but they were all secure. No way in through them and he refused to vandalize a property to gain entry.

"There's a basement window at the back that's not fastened," Mitchell said.

"How do you know that?"

"I scouted around before you guys got here."

"F..." His voice trailed off before the entire word spewed from his lips. "Better show us," Cooper conceded. He detested being beholding to Mitch on this, but despite that, the guy already knew a way into the house. Hopefully, the window would be large enough they could squeeze through it. If not, he'd send Nicole in first because she was the smallest. She could find her way from the basement to the door and let them in.

He soon found the window. Not only was it not latched, the glass was broken, too. Jagged shards remained in the frame. If they weren't careful, one of them could get hurt. No way would he send his sister through this point of entry. Cooper pulled a small flashlight from his back pocket, turned it on and concentrated the beam into the dark cavernous space under the house. "Looks like this might have been used as a coal chute back in the day," he said after an inspection. "Connor, you hold the window up and I'll drop down and see if there's some way of fastening it up from the inside."

"Be careful," Nicole said.

His lips tugged into a smile.

"I'll go," Mitch said. "I found it."

"You're not getting in there before me," Cooper said, pushing closer to the man.

"Fine. You don't have to be such a dickhead about it."

"Will you two let it go?" Nicole asked.

Cooper turned and lay on the ground, feet towards the house. Connor held the window up, and the man slithered through the opening on his belly.

Mitchell watched in awe at the ease with which Cooper entered the house. He was never that flexible. But now that the man was inside, would he come up and unlock the place, if he could, and let the rest of them inside? What if he was consigned to just the cellar? He patted his pockets. He didn't carry anything to help them get in through the door.

He stood bent over next to Nicole and, along with Connor, watched the beam of the flashlight move from side to side. It reminded him of a searchlight, like an airport beacon.

"I found the steps," Cooper yelled from within.

It shouldn't be much longer; they should all be in the house. Still, a stair tread giving out when stepped on would be satisfying. Not one near the top to cause serious injury, but a lower one. Something had changed in Cooper over the years. Before they began their urban exploration activities. Mitchell still got on well with Connor and Nicole, but his friendship with the elder twin soured. Cooper had become overly protective of Nicole, too. Maybe that was it? Back off. Don't date my baby sister. If he'd come out and say it, Mitch would know for sure if that was the reason for the shift in their friendship dynamic.

Chapter Four

OCTOBER 15, 2022

Cooper shone the beam of his flashlight around the room. Cobwebs stretched between the beams and down the walls. This space was likely twenty by twenty, give or take. No doors into other subterranean rooms. The footprint for the entire building was way larger than this. When his light showed the stairs, he worked his way up the basement steps, stopping on each tread to test its strength, and batting the offending abandoned spider webs away from this face. He wasn't taking any chances.

On a previous exploration, the floorboards of the property gave way under his foot and he was injured. His lower right leg still bore the scars of that misadventure. A crooked scar ran up his calf muscle from the jagged wood. He should have sought medical attention straight away, but his stubbornness and his pride refused to let him. It wasn't until hours later, when he and his siblings were on their way home, that he finally succumbed to the pain and let himself be driven to the hospital rather than his apartment.

When he reached the top of the steps and opened the door on the main floor, out of habit, he reached for the light switch, which was one of the old knob and tube push button ones. Surprisingly, the power hadn't been disconnected. How long had this building been abandoned? He recalled Connor saying it was converted to a hotel in the 1940s but didn't say if or how long it remained occupied after the hoteliers walked away from it. A thin layer of dust covered all the flat surfaces. The wallpaper peeled in the corners. But the lights worked.

Bang!

Cooper whipped around. It sounded like a gunshot from somewhere within the walls of the structure. But he was the only person inside. Maybe it was a door slamming? A gust of wind through a broken window on an upper floor on the other side of the building? The place creeped him out, which was a first. He'd explored abandoned houses in far worse condition than this one and they never affected him like this. He heaved a sigh when he saw the corridor that led to the entrance. Rather than lose face and let the others see he'd been spooked by something, Cooper took a few deep breaths, then strolled to the entryway and opened the door.

"Hey, bro. You look like you saw a ghost," Connor said. "What do you guys think?"

"You are kinda pale," said Nicole.

Connor tipped his head back. A gigantic crystal chandelier hung from a decorative ceiling medallion above him. A matching one dangled near the foot of the stairs where the corridor branched off to the right.

"Did you guys hear a door slam while you waited for me to let you in?" Cooper asked. "From in here, it sounded like a gunshot; it was that loud."

"No," the three answered in unison.

Suddenly, the crystals in the light fixture above Connor began to tinkle. The vibration and noise from the facets increased as if someone were jumping up and down on the floor above. He stepped back, confident that the whole thing would come crashing down on top of him. "What the ... ?"

The others had backed away, too, as if they expected the same eventuality as he did. As quickly as the disturbance started, it dissipated. Weird.

"Wind, maybe?" Nicole suggested.

"From where?"

"Don't know."

"Coop, you think this and your experience are why the hoteliers bailed on the place?"

"Not sure, Conn, but it does make you wonder."

"What's your take on this, Mitch?" Connor asked. So far, he was the only one who hadn't spoken since they entered the house.

"There has to be a logical explanation. The wind blew through a broken window. Maybe it slammed a door upstairs. Maybe it made the chandelier rattle. Why? Do you think this place might be haunted? That some ghost from the past is trying to put us off exploring here?"

To make his point that there was a logical explanation for the events, Mitchell walked to the main door, opened it and slammed it shut as hard as he could. The glass in the door rattled. The chandelier rattled and the heavy door banged closed loudly. "See? Nothing but our imaginations."

Should he dismiss the two prior events so quickly? He didn't believe in the supernatural. That was a load of bullshit. Séances, ghosts, and mediums who professed to be able to talk to the dearly departed. When you were dead, you were dead. Nothing more. Death was a permanent sleep. Your body was either stuck in the ground or cremated and either placed in an urn on someone's mantle or buried.

This house, mansion, villa, whatever you wanted to call it, was bricks and mortar. Well, in this case, granite and mortar. The only thing to be afraid of here was unsafe structure, and that didn't seem to be the case. Kembleford Manor seemed to be solid.

Nicole had stopped taking photos and sat on the staircase with her sketchbook. He admired her artistic ability, whether it was her eye for framing scenes to create the most impact or her drawing talent. Some of her sketches were so well done, if you didn't look closely, you'd swear they were photographs.

Mitchell walked down the hall and sat beside her on the third step from the bottom. "Can I see?"

She turned the book towards him. The drawing

was of the room they were in from their current perspective. The two doors leading to rooms on the right side of the corridor. The hallway and the two doors at the end. One that separated the main part of the house from the vestibule and the outer door. For the most part, the image was clear and well defined. "What's this cloudy area?" he asked.

"Don't you see it?"

"No. What am I supposed to be seeing?"

"It-it's hard to explain. I think it's an aura, but I don't know who or what it belongs to."

"What sort of nonsense is that? An aura."

"You have one around you, too. Everyone does."

"Okay, so what's my so-called *aura* doing?" Mitchell made air quotes around the word.

"Right now, it's very dark. Almost black. That's not a good thing. If I remember correctly, it means selfish and unkind."

"So what colour is this aura in your sketch?"

"Pink."

"Why not just use your camera and take a picture?"

"Because the camera won't pick it up."

Nicole flipped to a blank page in her sketchbook and moved into the room to the right of the stairs. The door was open a few inches, so she pushed it wide enough that she could gain entry. It was a formal living room decorated in the early 1900s style. A huge chandelier hung from a decorative medallion at the centre of the ceiling. Ornate wall sconces were at the sides of the windows, the fireplace, and between the bookcases.

This would have served as the lounge for guests. The huge bay window faced the circular drive. Heavy burgundy velvet drapes framed it. Funny, there wasn't as much dust as she had expected to find in a house that had been empty for this length of time. Did someone come in and clean periodically? If so, would she and her fellow explorers be caught out in the house?

She raised her DSLR camera to her eye and photographed the room from every possible angle. When she lowered the camera, the same pink aura she saw in the hallway manifested itself above a chair. A loud gasp escaped her lips. Nicole removed the pencil from above her ear and sketched the vision in front of her furiously.

"You okay in here?" Cooper asked as he reached the door.

"Y-yes." She turned back towards the chair and the aura had disappeared. Frightened? Not so much. Startled, more like. Nicole shuffled out of the room past her brother and walked towards the next door on the same side of the hallway as the one she just exited.

The brass doorknob gleamed. Usually, in time, the brilliance tarnished. There had to be a cleaner employed to look after the place. She turned the knob. This door opened into a dining room. A huge wooden table was surrounded by ten chairs, four on each side and one at each end. A fireplace filled the outside wall between two windows, one of which was in an alcove. Another chandelier provided the main lighting for the room, with wall sconces adding additional light. Again, she photographed the room from all angles.

"Hey you guys, come check this out," Connor called out from another ground floor room. He was standing behind the mahogany desk when the others joined him. "The heart of the Kembleford Manor empire?"

"You mean where deals were made over cigars and whisky?" Nicole asked.

"Could be. I can see old man Kembleford sitting here and his business associates in these chairs." He pointed to the two leather armchairs facing the huge desk. "This cabinet here would have held his collection of booze and glasses. You don't suppose there's still some stashed, do you?" Connor opened the cabinet, but to his disappointment, the cupboard was empty of alcohol. Some crystal old-fashioned glasses sat on the upper shelf. A decanter of the same pattern on the bottom one.

A huge painting of a man in hunting garb and his faithful dog, holding a dead pheasant in its mouth, hung on the wall above the liquor cabinet. Was this the man himself? A seasoned hunter who loved nothing better than a day out in the wild with his dog and rifle? Nowadays, you had to wear blaze orange when you were out hunting. This man was dressed in tweed, so the portrait was of the same era as the house.

Nicole's gaze was fixed on the desk. He could tell from the angle she held the sketchbook she was drawing the room — at least that side of it — as long as he didn't make it into the artwork. Normally, her interest lie in the furnishings and the decorative touches, although he had found himself immortalized before in her work.

A chill filled the room, as if a window was open and the cold wind blew in. Connor turned towards the windows and checked. All closed and secure. Imagination. Had to be. This place had to be at least a century older than any of the other abandoned places he and his siblings explored. Maybe it was the style of the building that made it seem that old. They'd never been inside any place of this grand a scale before. It was only normal that a few strange things might take place. Isn't that what drove the hoteliers out? Strange phenomena. Things that go bump in the night.

Nicole left the office room hurriedly. That chill. Was she the only one who felt it? The way Connor had spun around and checked the windows said that he did, too. Her sketch showed nothing untoward. The photos wouldn't show anything either. Something in there was wrong but she couldn't put her finger on it.

She started up the staircase to the second level of the abandoned mansion. As she ascended the stairs, the air suddenly chilled, and something moved by, jostled her, pushing her against the wall and forcing a startled yelp from her. Nicole dropped onto the step closest and sketched out this bizarre encounter. It wasn't Mitch or either one of her brothers. It was a man dressed in a black suit and white shirt, black waistcoat, and black tie. Clothing styled from about one hundred years ago. None of them were dressed in that way. And none of them were transparent. It had to be the guys playing a trick on her. After all, they were pranksters.

"Connor, Cooper, Mitch, not funny, guys." Nicole stared at the location where the apparition stood. "I mean it guys, this isn't funny."

"What's going on, sis?" Connor asked as he poked his head out of the room his sister had just vacated.

The ghost or whatever it was faded away.

"*Yesterday, upon the stair,*" she whispered.

"What are you talking about?" Cooper asked as he joined her in the corridor.

Nicole's eyes remained transfixed where the ghost-like being vanished into thin air.

Yesterday, upon the stair,
I met a man who wasn't there!
He wasn't there again today,
I wish, I wish he'd go away!

"What gibberish is that you're spouting?"

"It's not gibberish. It's the first stanza of the poem *Antigonish* by William Hughes Mearns. Don't you guys know nothin'?"

Chapter Five

OCTOBER 15, 2022

Still shaken by her experience on the stairs, Nicole hesitated about exploring the rest of the mansion. She wouldn't be going by herself. Her camera dangled around her neck. The pencil she'd used to sketch the ghost of the man who bumped into her was tucked behind her ear. Her book of drawings was under her arm.

"Want me to go with you, Nicki?" Mitch asked.

"Sure. As long as you wouldn't rather be doing something else."

"I admit I do have an ulterior motive."

"Such as? Maybe having your wicked way with me in one of the bedrooms up here?" Nicole smiled and winked at him.

Mitchell paled. "N-not that I would refuse such an opportunity, should it arise, but that's not it."

She'd never seen him lost for words in all the years she'd known him. What she said was meant as a joke. Although, she did find him attractive. "Not even being my knight in shining armour and saving a poor, wee damsel in distress?"

"I could do that if the need arose. I was thinking of staying out of your brother's way. Cooper is being a jerk."

"Being himself, you mean."

"Your words, not mine."

Nicole looped her arm around Mitchell's. "Come

on. Let's check out what's on the next level."

Halfway up, the staircase turned one hundred and eighty degrees. When they stepped onto the upper level of the house, Nicole heard a faint noise. "Do you hear that?"

"No. What?"

"It sounds like crying."

She walked to the door of the closest room and put her ear against it. Nothing. She moved on to the next room. Again, the same result. Directly across the hall on the landing from the steps, the sound became louder. Gut-wrenching sobs came from behind the wall. Where was the door to this room? Did you have to go through another to get here?

"You don't hear that."

"No."

"It's in here. A girl, woman. Definitely a female, and she's crying her eyes out."

Nicole shrugged her backpack to the floor and rooted through it. She pulled out a notebook and a roll of tape. "We're going to tape a piece of paper to every window on this level, then we'll go outside and see if they're all marked. I read somewhere they did this at Glamis Castle in Scotland, except they hung towels in all the windows. Come on." She dragged him back to the first bedroom.

"What do you want me to do?" Mitch asked.

Nicole handed him the roll of tape and then tore a sheet from her notebook and handed it to him. "You tape the paper to the window. In about the middle of it."

"It's a bay window here. On all three panes or just the middle one."

"All."

They repeated the process throughout every room on the second floor. Mitch would have liked to spend more time in each room, but Nicki was on a mission. If what she said about the Scottish castle proved true here, maybe he would get the opportunity to explore that level and the smaller one above it.

When they finished with the last window, they

descended the back stairs and into the long corridor that ran towards the front of the house.

Connor was exiting one of the rooms along this hall when they arrived. "What's up with you guys? You look like ... never mind that, if Cooper thinks you were, look out."

"Nothing like that," Mitch said. "Come outside with us. We've just taped a sheet of paper in every window on the second floor. Nicki, here, thinks there's another room up there but damned if I can see how to access it."

"And, how is taping paper to a window going to prove that?"

"Dear brother, sometimes you really can be thick. If there's a window with no paper in it, that proves my point."

"Let's go through here. There are doors off the conservatory," Mitch said.

Once outside, they walked far enough away from the house they'd have perfect views of the upstairs windows. Every single one on this side of the house had been marked. Again, all were marked in the two rooms with the bay windows. The three continued around the house.

"Look! Up there. In the window over the office. There's no paper stuck to the glass. We did every room up there. Didn't we, Mitch," Nicole said.

"Yes."

"Looks like you missed one," said Connor. He smirked.

"We didn't miss it because we didn't have access to that room."

"What do you mean?"

"Come back in and upstairs with us."

"Don't you want to check the rest first?" Mitch asked.

"No. That's the room where I heard the woman sobbing."

Her brother frowned.

Nicole raced back into the house and up the

stairs. Her theory was proven correct. There was a secret room. Well not so secret anymore. Not after the experiment she and Mitch conducted. She was breathless by the time she reached the top of the stairs.

Footsteps sounded from behind. Connor and Mitchell joined her. "You guys took your sweet time. Straight across there. Somewhere in that wall should be a door. But there isn't."

Connor strode to the location his sister indicated. The wall was decorated exactly the same as the rest of the ones in the hallway on this level.

Connor tapped on the wall. Solid sounding enough. He continued tapping as he moved towards the corner and the doorway into the adjacent room. The sound changed. It became hollow.

"Come here, you guys. Listen to this."

When Mitchell and Nicole were at his side, he continued. "It sounds like there used to be a door there at one time, but for whatever reason, it was filled in," Connor said and then he pointed to the floor. "No baseboard. They closed it off but never finished it entirely.

"Why would anyone want to do that?" Mitch asked.

"Why didn't I see that before? How did I miss it?" Nicole lamented. "It was behind this wall, I heard a woman crying. Sobbing actually. Gut-wrenching ones. But why would they do this?"

"Maybe the hoteliers blocked it in because no one would stay in that room," Connor said.

"A ghostly lady. Lamenting the death of a loved one?" Nicole suggested.

"This house is weird. I'll give you that, sis, but I don't think it's haunted."

"Can we get in there?" Mitch asked.

Connor ran his hands along the wall searching for something that would unlock the secret door. "Don't think so." Whatever the reason for sealing the room, it wasn't going to be discovered by them. The only way to do it would be to rip the wallpaper off and physically destroy it. That was over and above their remit as urban explorers. Actions of that sort boiled down to vandalism.

"So, we'll never know why," Nicole said as she heaved a heavy sigh.

Nicole sat on the floor with her sketchbook. She removed the pencil from behind her ear but the image she wanted to portray refused to manifest itself. If only there was some way she could comfort the grieving woman, whoever she was. Did these ghostly encounters have anything to do with the Kembleford family? Was someone trying to send a message?

Whatever the reason, whoever the person or persons, she wasn't going to discover their identities today. At least not now. Since she couldn't get an image of the person in her head, Nicole sketched the corridor with particular emphasis on the closed-in doorway. Why hadn't she noticed the lack of baseboard? She'd had her ear to the wall in that very spot. Distracted by the sounds coming from the other side? Possibly. The song *Crying Game* popped into her head. She was only a little girl when Boy George recorded it. How did she know the artist? Did her mother or father play it on cassette or record? All she recalled of the song was his haunting, and melancholy voice. Haunted and melancholy suited this old house.

At least they hadn't experienced anything Uber scary. But they weren't done yet. There was still plenty of time for that to happen. Mind you, some people might have thought Nicole's experiences were terrifying. It all came down to your personal level of fright.

Nicole moved slowly throughout the rest of the upstairs, alternating between taking photos and drawing. At the end of the long narrow hallway, she ascended another staircase which led to a further level. The ceilings up here were sloped so she had to duck in places to get through. It looked like it had once been an attic and later converted to living space.

So far this third level of the house was the only place she'd not had any strange encounters. Was that because the ghosts who she felt and saw on the lower levels never came up here? Was it added at a later date? It would be worth looking into once she returned home. There had to be more than just the website Connor showed them. Still, she sketched as well as photographed all the rooms before returning to the main level of the house.

"I don't know about you guys, but I've seen enough inside. Why don't we scout out the grounds? See what there is there. Maybe even head over to the lumber company. It's close by, isn't it Conn?" Cooper asked.

Connor pulled his cell phone out of his back pocket and punched some buttons. "Yeah. Looks like it should be over there going by the map." He turned his phone so his brother could see.

"Close enough to walk or do we need to take my SUV?"

"Walkable, I think. As long as the tree cover isn't too dense. It doesn't look like it from here."

Cooper concurred with his brother. He'd rather leave his vehicle where it was and explore on foot. There would be less chance of them being spotted that way. No sense drawing attention to yourself if you don't have to. His olive green clothing was dust and cobweb covered from sliding in through the basement window. He brushed himself off as best he could and the brothers started towards the mill.

"Should we let Nicki and Mitch know where we're going? Something could happen over there, or we get lost trying to get there or back."

"Good idea, Conn." Cooper pulled out his phone and composed a message to his sister. He didn't care about telling Mitchell of their whereabouts, but if the worst-case scenario were to happen, and Nicole couldn't find them, he didn't want her to worry.

Connor and I heading to lumber mill. He hit send.

"Okay, let's go. I've texted Nicki," Cooper said. He was returning his phone to his back pocket when it vibrated.

Be careful. Let me know what you find.

Cooper started out in the direction of the Kembleford Lumber Company, or whatever it was called. Did it even still exist? The place could be long gone by now. Maybe, it was still in use as a retail store similar to Home Depot or Rona. They wouldn't necessarily be sourcing local wood, but having it trucked in, instead.

Chapter Six

SEPTEMBER 27, 1891

With James sleeping and Albert off in another part of the hotel, Patience took advantage of the few moments of quiet so she could write a letter to her mother. She sat down at the table by the window, readied her pen and took her writing paper from the box she'd brought it in to Canada.

How many thousands of miles was she from home? Their passage across the ocean took ten days. Then, they spent one night in Quebec City before making the short voyage to the port of Montreal.

Below the room, horse-drawn carriages traversed the cobbled streets. The echo of the horses' hooves wafted through the open window.

27 September, 1891

Dearest Mother,

We have arrived safely in Canada. It was a very long ten days at sea with an infant to care for and an extremely seasick husband. The seas were terribly rough for a few days shortly after we sailed from Liverpool. I thought the ship might capsize. Captain Ritchie assured me this was not the case; however, he did suggest we didn't venture out of our cabin until calmer seas graced us with their presence.

The RMS Parisian was more than I could have

imagined. Our cabin was adequate. Much better than the third-class ones but less opulent than those in first-class. There was plenty of room for the three of us. We've made a bed for wee James using one of the bureau drawers. He seems quite content. And no, mother, he's not sleeping in the bureau. We've taken the drawer out and placed it next to our bed.

I'm writing this from the hotel we're spending the next two nights in before we board a train to take us to our final destination. From the window, I can look out over the harbour and watch the ships offloading their cargo.

I will write more once we arrive and are settled.
Your loving daughter,

Patience

When her husband returned, she would take the letter downstairs to reception and have them mail it for her. Hopefully, the letter wouldn't take too long to reach her mother back in England.

Chapter Seven

OCTOBER 1, 1891

The compartment they had on the train didn't have berths, so they had to sleep lying across the seats. There was no provision for James, either. Patience held him to her chest. On one of the rounds the conductor made, he saw their predicament and returned with a box where the baby could sleep. It wasn't ideal, but it worked. And it was no worse than the bureau drawer they had used on the ship and in their hotel room.

Patience dozed in her seat, the swaying back and forth of the carriage as the train sped along the tracks, made her drowsy. When she wasn't dozing, she watched the passing scenery.

She was thrilled to get off the train when it stopped at their destination in Pike Falls. It might have only been two and a half days, but it had been tiring.

Patience was in awe of the sight before her. Never had she seen such a grand house. There were some similar in Scotland she'd seen on family visits as a child, but nothing like it where she lived in Market Rasen, Lincolnshire. The house she lived in with Albert was a tenement house. Two up, two down, and an outdoor toilet in the back garden.

She entered the front door. Ornate chandeliers hung from the ceiling. The doors and woodwork were stained a rich, dark brown. They'd been polished and shone. Delicate pale pink flowers adorned the wallpaper.

Patience opened the first door on her left. It was a formal dining room. The same attention to detail prevailed in there as in the main hallway. She and Albert had sold all their furniture before they left England. They had nothing that would suit such a grand house.

She went from room to room, then down the long corridor towards the back of the house. An enormous kitchen stood on one side, but what surprised her the most was the indoor bathroom, complete with sink, roll-top bath and toilet. No more having to go out the back door into a cold outhouse.

On one of the days they were laid over in Montreal, they went furniture shopping. Arrangements had been made for their purchases to be shipped to them by rail, and they would arrive on the freight cars of the mixed train they booked from Montreal to Pike Falls.

As if the thought of furnishings conjured them up, heavily laden horse-drawn carts entered the yard. Excited by the sight, she dashed outside to meet them.

Late that night, after the furniture had been installed in their proper rooms and they'd managed to have a bite to eat, Patience sat down and wrote to her mother.

1 October, 1891

Dearest Mother,

We have arrived at our new home. It's a grand stone manor house with bay windows on the front aspect and along the one side. There is even a tower between the front windows. I have yet to enter it as it's been a time getting the rest of the house in order.

I have a room set up as a nursery for James, and once he's a bit older, we'll move him into a bigger, more boyish room than his current accommodations.

Albert has purchased the lumber mill and the house from the previous owner. I love this beautiful old place. It's reminiscent of the manor houses we saw on trips into Scotland. The grounds are vast. There's even a boathouse at the water. I've not ventured down there yet. The weather hasn't been the best to be out and about with a tiny baby.

I'm told that the gardens are a riot of colours in the spring and summer, but now that autumn is here, and we're in a far more harsh climate than you are at home in Lincolnshire, the vibrant hues of earlier in the year are muted.

Winters can be quite harsh, and we could receive our first snowfall of the season soon. In a strange sort of way, I'm looking forward to it. I wasn't sure how I would feel being so far away from you, but Canada — at least Pike Falls — seems to be a friendly place, so I think we'll be just fine.

Albert wants to host some area businessmen and their wives to a Christmas soiree nearer the time. This house is so big, I shouldn't have any problem finding the room.

I'm looking to hire a Maid of All Work. Albert says we need at least one maid, if not more. We didn't have one back home in England, so I don't see why we need one now. I think he's trying to fit in, or perhaps rise above, his industry peers. I just hope he doesn't get in over his head. You know how he gets carried away.

I'll close this letter for now, Mother. I trust you and Father are well. I send my love to both of you.

Your loving daughter,

Patience

Chapter Eight

"**M**ary." Walter stood behind his wife. "Will you please hurry? We can't keep the people waiting."

"Do calm down, Walter. We've got plenty of time."

Walter paced back and forth. This was a huge day for him. For his entire family. It had to be perfect. He had longed to have his own business for years. His father, before him, ran a successful bakery. He remembered his childhood delivering bread to the faithful customers who couldn't leave their homes for one reason or another. He was an eight-year-old boy when the war broke out. Within months, things changed. His father could no longer get sufficient supplies. People had no money to buy what meagre baked goods the man could turn out. To survive, animals were slaughtered for food and to preserve what grain supplies were available.

Wiesbaden, where his father's bakery was, didn't suffer as severely as nearby Frankfurt in the bombing raids, but it was close enough that planes flying overhead at all hours of the day and night were heard. With the business suffering because of the economic hardships due to the war, his parents packed him and his younger brother up and booked passage to North America on an ocean liner. His mother was terrified to sail across the ocean. Titanic hit an iceberg and sank. Lusitania was torpedoed. Would that happen to their ship, too? He and Friedrich thought of it as an adventure.

Now, as he stood in the bedroom, he would share with his wife, the trials and tribulations of his past made him the man he was today. The man holding a grand opening for the hotel he had dreamt of owning since his arrival in Canada. It wasn't a large hotel. More of a guesthouse. Some of the bedrooms had en-suites, while others shared a bathroom. Still, he'd done the work himself. Mary had looked after the decorating. Much of the hotel remained as it was when it was the private home of Albert and Patience Kembleford. There really wasn't much to be done. Mostly, minor repairs and cleaning. The house had sat empty for over thirty years since the bank had foreclosed on the home and the nearby lumber mill.

Mary applied a slash of red lipstick and then blotted it with a tissue. Women's rituals, when it came to their appearance, baffled him. Why did they have to wear makeup when they were perfectly acceptable without it? She turned on the stool in front of the dressing table.

"How do I look?"

"Beautiful as always, my dear. Beautiful as always." Walter put his hand on the small of her back and walked her out of the room.

Downstairs, things were chaotic. Movers were bringing in their furniture. "No. That goes in the large room off the kitchen. In there." Mary pointed as she spoke to the men holding a large china cabinet. If it weren't for Grace's breathing problems, they would have stayed in the house from the beginning, but the dust set off a severe asthma attack, and the young girl ended up spending a few days in the local hospital.

Now, everything was spotless, and the woodwork and floors gleamed. Rugs were kept to a minimum, at least in the rooms the family would occupy. Grace had the small bedroom over the one that would be their snug. From what she recalled from their viewing of the property, that room was the one Albert Kembleford used as his office. The check-in desk was in the main corridor. Walter had built it from scratch — it and the cubby holes on the wall for room keys and messages for guests.

From her vantage point, a group of people gathered near the side of the property became visible. The moving truck blocked part of the view. It was the last-minute rush before they could relax and enjoy showing off their hard work to the world. The people of Pike Falls, at least. They'd been accepted here, unlike in her hometown, where the locals had shunned them because of her husband's nationality. Even her father hated Germans. He'd never forgiven her for marrying one, despite giving his blessing for the marriage. It was such a relief to come to a town where it didn't matter.

The grandfather clock by the main staircase chimed twelve o'clock. Still, an hour to go before the mayor and other dignitaries would arrive for the official ribbon cutting. Walter had been on edge and worried since he woke up. It was cutting it fine, but it would all work out in the end.

Mrs. Pritchard, the landlady at the boarding house where they'd stayed while working on the hotel, had been an absolute angel, especially after Grace's hospitalization. The woman insisted the little girl stay with her while Mary and Walter worked on refurbishing the hotel. She'd never be able to repay the woman for her kindness.

Mary smoothed the front of her shirtwaist dress and strode out to see how much was left to do before the big event.

"That's us done, lady. The last load is indoors," one mover said.

"Thank you so much. I know it was a lot of work. Heavy work."

"That's what we do, ma'am." Sweat dripped from the other man's brow, and he pulled out a colourful handkerchief and wiped his forehead with it.

"Let me get you some lemonade. You look like you could use it."

"That would be nice, ma'am."

"Wait right here." Mary retreated to the kitchen and poured two tall glasses of the refreshing drink. This room was her favourite in the entire house. Her domain. Even though Walter's father was a baker by trade, poor Walter couldn't boil water. He was totally useless in the kitchen. God love him.

"Here you are, gentlemen." Mary handed each one a glass. "I assume my husband has looked after the financial side of the business?"

"Yes, ma'am, he did. Very generous he was."

"I'm glad. Don't let me keep you. I'm sure you have other customers today since it's the last day of the month."

Mary waved them off and returned to the kitchen. Mrs. Pritchard had arrived and was busy arranging the hors d'oeuvres on serving platters. This was another reason why she'd never be able to repay the woman's kindness.

Grace skipped into the kitchen with her china doll, Clara, clutched to her chest. Walter's parents had brought it to Canada when they left Germany. The doll was passed down to her when they were blessed with a granddaughter. Only since they moved to Pike Falls did the little girl carry the doll with her everywhere she went. Perhaps she hadn't adjusted to the move north. It had been an upheaval for everyone. They couldn't stay in the house while they worked on it because of Grace's asthma attack. Mrs. Pritchard had appointed herself a grandmother to Grace, which helped them immensely while they worked on converting the manor house to a hotel.

"Grandma Pritchard, Clara wants to know when we can eat. There's so much food," Grace said.

"This food is for the reception, dear. But I'll get you a soft molasses cookie. Will that work?"

"Yes, please. Clara, too."

"Yes, dear. Clara, too."

Walter entered the kitchen as Grace was asking about food. He didn't like his daughter calling the Pritchard woman Grandma Pritchard. She wasn't her grandmother. Still, he couldn't deny that the woman had bonded with the child and looked after her so he and Mary could be here. Grace's severe asthma attack and subsequent hospitalization frightened him as much as it did his wife. Thankfully, there were no lasting effects, and his little girl was fit as a flea.

"How's Daddy's little angel?" he asked when he squatted before her.

"Clara and I are hungry, and Grandma Pritchard is getting us molasses cookies."

"You and Clara stay clean now. The ribbon cutting for our grand opening isn't far off." He stood and ruffled Grace's hair.

"Why do we have to cut a ribbon to live here?"

Walter paused. It was an excellent question and one that deserved an answer. How do you word it so a seven-year-old could understand? "Well, sweetie, we're opening our home as a hotel so other people can come and stay here when they're on holiday."

"Why?"

"It's something I've always wanted to do. My father — your grandfather — owned a bakery in Germany before we came to Canada."

"You can't cook, Daddy." Grace giggled.

"I know. But I can do things with my hands, and love meeting people. So, I let your mother look after the cooking, and I do the things I'm good at, like building things and gardening."

"But if people come here, what about Grandma Pritchard?"

"We won't be taking people away from her. The folks who stay there work up here. So Mrs. Pritchard's boarding house is their home. People will stop here when they're travelling. Maybe only stay one night. Maybe stay a week or longer."

Grace nodded; although Walter wasn't sure how much of what he said, she understood. He didn't want to talk down to his daughter. She was an intelligent girl.

"Mayor Stevens has arrived," Mary said when she returned to the kitchen. "Some of the other guests are here as well."

"We can't keep them waiting."

Chapter Nine

NOVEMBER 4, 1892

Patience was exhausted after the long labour she went through giving birth to her second child. James had been much easier in that he came quickly. Although Ophelia was born on the third, she had been in labour for over twenty hours before her daughter saw fit to enter the world. The midwife was a godsend and kept her calm throughout. At one point, Patience panicked. The labour should have been shorter. There had to be something wrong. Nothing wrong in that sense. Ophelia was a big baby. Bigger than James. No wonder it took so long.

She finally felt up to sitting at her table by the window. A letter to her mother was in order.

4 November, 1892

Dearest Mother,

It's a girl! She was born yesterday, 3 November, and is perfect. Ten fingers, ten toes, blue eyes, and a head of curly brown hair. I know she'll lose some, if not it all like James did. We've named her Ophelia, after your mother. Would it be impertinent of me to say she sounds just like your mother when she cries the house down for her feed? I think Father would find my statement amusing.

Albert insists we hire a Nursery Maid now that we

have a small boy and an infant daughter in the house. I think Matilda, our Maid of All Work, and I can look after two children and the house, but he insists. I believe I told you about hiring a maid. Did I tell you we had?

Our letters take so long to get to and fro; sometimes, I don't know if you even receive mine. I know your rheumatism makes it hard to hold a pen for any length of time, so I don't expect you to answer all of them. Still, writing them makes me feel closer to you.

I hope you and Father are well as we are here.

You are always in my thoughts.

Your loving daughter,

Patience

Chapter Ten

JUNE 30, 1947

Walter ushered his wife and daughter to the area at the circular driveway where the ceremonial ribbon cutting would take place. Sweat dripped from his armpits, soaking his white shirt. At least his suit jacket covered the wet patches. It wasn't an overly hot day, so his perspiration had to be caused by his nerves.

Mayor Stevens was a formidable presence. Tall and rotund, he commanded respect, or fear, from those he encountered. Other council members were there, plus reporters and photographers from the local newspaper and other area papers. Curious residents joined the group.

"Ladies and gentlemen," Mayor Stevens began, "it gives me great pleasure to welcome you to the grand opening of the Kembleford Manor Hotel. I give you the proprietors of the establishment, Walter and Mary Birkhoefer."

A round of applause went up from the gathered crowd.

"M-my wife and I thank you, Mayor Stevens," Walter replied. "We also thank everyone who has come out today." A hand touched his shoulder and he glanced to his left. Mary, who had worked alongside him from the beginning, gave it a gentle squeeze and smiled a reassuring smile.

"Many long hours went into the refurbishment, or

if you prefer, the restoration of this grand house. You'll soon be able to see the fruits of our labours. I don't know how many of you ever had the opportunity to visit the house when the Kemblefords owned it. We've kept it as it was then, but with added ... embellishments. It's a beautiful home, and we wanted to preserve it as much as possible, but with a few modern enhancements."

"Mr. Birkhoefer, James Clancy, Pike Falls Courier," a thin blondish man with a nicotine-stained moustache said. "Can you tell us why you moved away from your home in Quabbinville?"

Walter's German accent came through stronger now. "Unfortunately, people have long memories. My parents, brother, and I had long since emigrated to Canada. We left Germany in 1916, long before Hitler and his atrocities. I had many cousins, aunts and uncles who remained in our homeland. Sadly, I have no idea what's become of them."

The reporter spoke again. "What do you have to say about the Kembleford curse?"

"I don't know what you mean. I've never heard of it."

"Albert Kembleford shot himself in this very house. His eldest daughter, Ophelia, also committed suicide. She had a daughter born prematurely and stillborn. Does it not make you wonder what you've gotten you and your family into, sir?"

"I don't believe in such tittle-tattle."

"Without any further ado, I think it's time you cut the ribbon on your hotel opening, don't you?" Mayor Stevens said and handed Walter a massive pair of ceremonial scissors.

"Thank you, sir." Walter positioned the shears and, as he sliced through the fabric, said, "Ladies and gentlemen gathered here today, I give you the Kembleford Manor Hotel."

A round of applause echoed through the gathering. Flashbulbs popped, and the bright flashes forced Walter to blink even though they were outside. For a few minutes afterwards, he still had spots before his eyes.

Once he'd recovered, he said, "And now, if you follow me, my wife, and daughter, you can have a tour before convening in the formal dining room on the ground floor for refreshments."

It was later than usual before Mary settled Grace into her bed in the room over the snug.

"But I'm not tired, Mother," the little girl protested.

"It's been a long day for all of us. You're still keyed up from all the excitement. You and Clara need to get a good night's sleep." Mary was ready to fall into her bed.

"Will Daddy come up and say good night?"

More stalling tactics.

"Yes. I'll send him up."

Mary switched off the light and drew the door shut but left it open about an inch, so the light from the hall filtered into her daughter's room.

As she descended the stairs, she met Walter on his way up. "Grace is waiting for you to say goodnight, dear," she said.

"I hope she likes her room. It's smaller than most, but I wanted to keep the larger ones for the paying guests."

"I'm sure it will be fine." Mary leaned over and kissed her husband's cheek before carrying on downstairs.

"How's Daddy's little angel now?" Walter asked when he sat on the edge of Grace's bed.

"I'm all right. I don't want to go to sleep. This room scares me."

"Why do you say that? What's so scary?"

"I don't know. It just makes me scared."

Walter was puzzled at his daughter's reaction to her bedroom. Had she told her mother the same thing? He would mention it to Mary when he joined her in the snug.

"Would you like me to leave the light on for you?"

"Yes, please."

"Fine, then." Walter kissed Grace on the forehead and adjusted the blankets to cover her and her doll. "Good night. I love you."

"I love you, too, Daddy."

Walter paused in the doorway, turned and blew Grace a kiss before he made his way downstairs to the snug.

Walter removed his suit jacket, folded it. and draped it over the back of the wingback chair near the bay window in the snug before he sank into the seat. A round side table stood nearby with a tray holding a whisky decanter and four glasses. He stood and poured himself a measure of the amber liquid. Today had gone well. The family was moved into their new home. Their first guests were due the next day and they were booked until the weekend. He'd yet to pick up tourist information leaflets to have at reception, so he hoped the couple brought their own with them.

The restoration and conversion of the house to a hotel took most of his and his wife's time. He had no idea what there was in Pike Falls other than his hotel and Mrs. Pritchard's boarding house. The Pike River ran through the village, so fishing and boating were possible activities for his guests. A rail line ran parallel to the main road. He'd never noticed if there was a station or passenger service, for that matter. These were all minor details in the grand scheme of things.

Mary joined him at the window. Although not as large as the formal living room, this room had a coziness. There wasn't a fireplace but a cast iron radiator under the window instead.

"Would you care to join me in a drink, my dear?" he asked.

"Please." She shifted in the other wingback chair to accept the whisky. "I think today went extremely well, don't you, Walter?"

"Yes. It went down well, thanks to your organization. You ensured everything ran smoothly, from the movers to the food to the tour. I couldn't have done any of this without you."

Mary blushed and raised her glass in an unspoken toast.

"Has Grace said anything to you about her bedroom?"

"Other than it was the one she picked out because it was close to ours? No," she replied and set her glass on the table.

"I had an interesting conversation with her when I went up to tuck her in and say goodnight."

"Oh?"

"She said the room scared her. She couldn't say what it was about it. I left her light on. We can turn it out when we go to bed. She should be asleep by then."

"Maybe it's just the first night in the new house in her new room," Mary said. "I don't think there's anything to worry about."

Mary fell asleep almost as quickly as her head hit the pillow. Grace was fine when she checked in on her, so she turned the bedroom light off but left the door open. Walter had extinguished the one in the hall but left the one on in their room so she could see to find her way across the corridor.

Her husband's rhythmic soft snoring lulled her into unconsciousness. The peace was interrupted by a loud scream from Grace's room. She and Walter sat bolt upright. It came again. While it wasn't blood-curdling, it was a screech of terror.

They leapt out of bed and dashed to the room where the noise originated from. Grace sat up in bed, crying, "No, you can't have her. Clara is mine!" It looked like she was playing tug of war with an invisible entity. But that wasn't possible. There was no one else in the room. Grace's eyes were wide open but weren't focused on anyone. The little girl wasn't awake. They'd have to wake her carefully. She wasn't sleepwalking, but she was sleep something.

Mary crept to the bed and put her hand on Grace's shoulder. "Grace. It's your mother. Wake up," Mary whispered.

Grace blinked and looked around the room. Why were her parents here? This wasn't their bedroom.

"Are you okay, sweetheart?" Mary asked and sat on the bed beside her.

"Th-th-there was a l-lady in here. She t-tried to take Clara. Said she was her baby." Grace wrapped her arms around her mother and snuggled to her bosom.

"She's not here now, sweetie. You must have scared her away."

"Do you want your mother to stay with you?" Walter asked. "She'll protect you."

Grace held on tighter than before. "Y-yes, please."

"I will then," Mary said.

"If that lady comes back, will you make her go away?"

"Yes."

Grace shuffled over to the far side of the bed, so her mother could join her under the covers.

Chapter Eleven

Patience woke at about two-thirty that afternoon. She'd fallen asleep not long after giving birth to her second daughter. The labour wasn't as difficult or lengthy as when she had Ophelia, and this baby wasn't as big either. Lavinia decided to come into the world kicking and screaming around three o'clock in the morning. At first, when Patience woke, she wasn't sure if it was still the same day or possibly the next.

Matilda looked in on her after she woke and helped her to the table by the window so she could write to her mother and give her the wonderful news. Being New Year's Eve, her father likely celebrated down at the pub with his friends. Patience smiled when she recalled a night when she was a young girl and her father had drunk to excess and paraded around the house.

31 December, 1893

Dearest Mother,

It's another girl! In the early hours of this morning. It's now mid-afternoon, and I've taken myself to the table by the window so I can write this. Matilda is looking after me to ensure I don't overdo things. She's made me promise not to go back to bed without her help, and to that end, she has provided me with a bell to ring to summon her. I have a lovely cup of tea by my side. The view from this window on the last day of the year is spectacular. The ground is covered with snow. We have at least a foot of it. The sun is shining, and when it catches the ice crystals in the snow, they glitter like diamonds. And the sky! Not a cloud to be seen from my vantage point, and it's the bluest of blues.

We did hire a Nursery Maid after Ophelia's birth. She's still with us. Her name is Catherine Pritchard. Now, with another baby in the house, we'll definitely need the extra help.

Oh, the baby! I didn't tell you anything other than it was another girl and the time. We've named her Lavinia. She's the image of her older siblings right down to the dark curly hair. Was it you who told me the old wives' tale that babies are born at the same time they were conceived?

James and Ophelia are well. James is a big boy and likes to help his younger sister. She isn't always so receptive to his assistance and has been known to throw things at him, for which she's been reprimanded. Only last month, he was sporting a black eye from a battle with his sister.

I can't see Ophelia turning into a lady. She's more boyish than her brother. But maybe it's because of his influence. There aren't any children close by for them to mix with. Our house is outside the village so we don't get far when we're out taking the air. And now, with a newborn, we'll be staying even closer to home for a while.

Does Father still get silly on New Year's Eve? I remember sneaking out of my bedroom and sitting on the stairs, watching him. It was the only time I ever saw him take a drink. Then he'd be high-stepping around the room, waving his right hand in the air. I do miss seeing that. I'll have to hold that vision in my mind's eye.

I hope you and Father are well and that your rheumatism isn't bothering you too much in this colder weather.

Happy New Year!

Your loving daughter,

Patience

Chapter Twelve

OCTOBER 15, 2022

Nicole walked into the room where the huge mahogany desk was located. Presumably, it was a home office at one time. Working from home wasn't all that new a concept. Businessmen back in the day would take work home and sequester themselves in a quiet place to complete tasks that weren't done during working hours. This room was luxurious and well-appointed. The portrait was disarming, in that no matter where she stood in the room, the eyes followed her. Or at least they seemed to do that. It might have been her imagination.

She backed towards the door. "Mitch, are you in the house somewhere?"

Footsteps sounded above her.

"Mitch? Is that you clomping around upstairs?"

Still no answer. That same chill that filled the room before returned. Not just a cold chill. But icy and clammy. She turned her attention back to the desk. There slumped over the desk's surface was the figure of a man. It appeared to be the same one she encountered earlier on the stairs. A startled squeak escaped from her mouth.

Frightening? Yes. A threat to her safety? Doubtful. Nicole flipped to a fresh page in her sketchbook and worked frantically. She didn't dare move closer in case the apparition vanished. The image she worked on took shape. Body, desk, windows, wall. When she first entered the room, the wall to her right, except for peeling wallpaper was unblemished. Now, it was splattered with blood and, was that grey matter? Bits of the man's brains and skull fragments?

She turned and ran straight into Mitch.

"I heard you calling me. What's up?"

"Do you see it?" Nicole asked, her voice shaky.

"What am I supposed to be seeing?"

"At the desk. A body slumped over it. Part of his head splattered on the wall?" She didn't dare turn around. Her stomach lurched.

"Nothing like that. Just the room. The same as when we saw it before." Mitchell put his arms around her and pulled her close.

Why was she the only one who saw and heard these strange things? Were the spirits trying to channel themselves through her to tell or show her something? What happened within these walls all those years ago?

Nicole let Mitch lead her from the room and outside into the fresh air.

The cool air helped clear Nicole's head. Inside the house had been too much. She needed to get a grip. She clutched her sketchbook under her arm, turned around, and faced the house. In the room above where a previous resident committed suicide, a figure moved by the window. The room where she'd heard the crying. The one with no paper taped to the glass.

Now, a dark-haired woman in a long white dress — turn of the twentieth-century style — looked out. She held something in her arms, bundled in a light-coloured blanket. Was it a baby? Is that why she wept? "Mitch, do you see that?"

"What?"

"Up there. A woman is standing in the window. I'm sure of it." Nicole turned to a fresh page in her artist's book and began to draw.

It had to be her imagination. Or was it something more sinister? She was losing her mind.

Mitch worried about Nicole. In all the time he'd known her and her brothers, she wasn't one to see things that weren't there. She was always level-headed. Not prone to hysteria, if that's what you called her current mindset. He peered over her shoulder as the sketch took shape. It was a close-up of the window with enough of the outer wall for context. Off to the side, this dark-haired woman staring outside, Nicki claimed she saw, holding something in her arms. Tears streaked her face. Parts of the room that remained hidden from the home's interior showed through the transparent figure. Mitch blinked, thinking he was seeing things, but when he cast his eyes on the page, the vision was still there.

"When you're finished with that, do you want to check out the boathouse?" he asked.

At first, his suggestion was met with silence.

Finally, Nicole turned towards him. "How do you know there's a boathouse?"

"I told you guys I scouted around before you arrived. Did you forget?"

"Yeah, must have. Sorry. Let me text the guys and let them know where we're going." She pulled her phone out of her backpack and began to type with her thumbs. He stood beside her and watched her type the message.

Mitch & I are off to the boathouse. Will let you know what we find. How are things at the lumber mill?

"Okay, that's done. Lead on." Nicole shoved her phone back inside her rucksack.

"Not want to wait for a reply?"

"No. I'll check when we get there. Is it far?"

"Not too far. Come on."

Mitch laced his fingers through hers and steered her in the proper direction. Nothing was going to happen to Nicki on his watch. He didn't want to suffer Cooper's wrath if something happened to her. When they were younger, and she wanted to tag along with them, he never minded, even though her brothers objected. He stuck up for her. Shamed them into letting her come.

"There it is, just up there. You can barely see it

through the trees."

Nicole squinted, but she still couldn't see the structure. Was Mitch leading her on by telling her of a non-existent building? A few steps farther, one wall and a bit of the roof showed themselves through the trees. She felt safe when she was with him. She knew that he'd protect her, but what did she need protection from out here? There were no wild animals. Not even squirrels or chipmunks.

The raucous cawing from a crow broke the silence. That was the first birdsong she'd heard since they arrived. Soon after, another answered the call. Then another and another. Where were they? Ahead of them stood a tall spruce tree. One was at the top, on a branch barely large enough to support it. Lower in the tree was another. In a nearby clearing, two swaggered across the grass, stopping to stare at them as if to say, *you don't frighten me, humans, you inferior species.* Just then, the crow from the top of the tree swooped down to join the others. It flew so close to Nicole's head that she felt the wind it created.

She let go of Mitch's hand and began to draw. Both she and Mitch were in this sketch, drawn from behind. The enormous crow that flew over was beyond them but still in the air. From this angle, the birds on the ground weren't visible, but she captured more that were landing, having come from other directions. "Quite the welcoming committee," she said, although with the large birds staring at her, welcome was far from what she felt.

By now, the trees were less dense, and the boathouse was clear. The water, dark and still, beyond. A cold, clammy chill filled Nicole with dread when they approached the building. What next? She reached out for Mitch's hand. It was warm.

"You okay? Your hands are like ice," he said.

She nodded, but she was far from all right. This house. This property. They tormented her. None of the others seemed to be affected. Only her. Was she a means of exposing the tragic stories of events that took place here in the past? It seemed unlikely, but at this point, Nicole was willing to believe almost anything. Especially when it came to Kembleford Manor.

The boathouse wasn't locked. Mitch pushed the door open. Nicole planted her feet firmly on the ground and pushed back against him. "I-I can't go in there."

"Why?"

"Doesn't feel right. Something is wrong."

Mitch pulled out his phone and turned on its flashlight. He cast the beam around the inside and illuminated the interior bit by bit. "It's okay. You just have to stay close to the walls where the dock is."

Nicole crept forward but still remained outside. Evil? Or more tragedy?

The inky black water lapped against the building's supports, bringing with it the stench of dead fish.

"Gross," she said.

The torch reflected off the river. Then Nicole saw it. The figure of a young female clothed in a white dress, facedown, floating in the water, arms out to the side. The air between the body and the clothing made it billow into unnatural pillows. Who hadn't died in mysterious circumstances around this place? Nicole furiously sketched the scene in front of her. She never set foot inside the building.

"I'm going back." Nicole finished her sketch and packed her things inside her backpack. She hoped her brothers would be at the house waiting for hers and Mitch's return.

"You sure the lumber mill is this way?" Connor asked his brother. They'd taken a path across the clearing but now were back in trees and scrub.

Cooper pulled out his phone and pulled up the map he'd captured before they came to Pike Falls. Connor looked over his brother's shoulder. "It should be just ahead. The house was here," he said, pointing to a spot on the screen, "and the mill was straight ahead as the crow flies. Likely not much farther."

"Okay, but the trees are getting more dense. Maybe it would have made more sense to backtrack along the roads to get there."

"We'll keep going." Cooper shoved his phone into his back pocket and pushed ahead of his twin.

After about ten minutes of beating branches out of their way, the trees thinned out, and the mill came into view.

As they approached, vehicles were coming and going from the parking lot. A huge shed filled with milled timber stood behind the main building, which now operated as a retail outlet. The sign over the door proclaimed it to be McNaughton's Building Centre.

"Well, this isn't what we planned on seeing. I figured it was as abandoned as the house. Shit!"

"Can't always be right, Coop," Connor replied, slapping his brother's shoulder. "Head back to the house?"

"Nah, let's have a poke around here first. We can always let on we're looking for supplies for a project."

Connor rolled his eyes. This should be good. His brother might be computer savvy and great at designing and building websites, but he wouldn't know a two-by-four from a sledgehammer if it bit him in the arse or hit him over the head.

"Hey, what are you two doing lurking around over there?"

Busted. Well, might as well fess up for all the time it would take. Then talk their way out of a visit from the police.

"Here's your chance to show just how little you know about lumber," Connor said, slapping his brother's shoulder again.

"Sorry, we're looking for some help. I need some lumber for a project."

"Well you've come to the right place. Let's go into the office to discuss your materials list."

This was going to prove interesting. With any luck, between the two of them, they could spin a story that would sound plausible.

"That's just it. I don't know what I need. I can tell you what I want to create. If my sister was here, she could sketch it out so you had a visual. But she isn't, so you'll have to put up with my ramblings."

Connor had a hard time keeping a straight face. It was all he could do to not burst out laughing. If that happened, they'd be arrested for sure. He listened intently as Cooper related his vision and occasionally moved deftly to prevent a slap in the head from his brother's gesticulations.

In the meantime, the man who approached and questioned them outside was clicking away on a mouse. When Cooper finished, the man turned the screen so they could see his interpretation.

"That's it!"

"What's it? What in the hell is that?" Connor asked.

"The treehouse we never had as kids," Cooper said, winking.

"Really, sir? It doesn't look anything like a treehouse."

"Sure it does." Connor stepped up. This was going to be fun. "Right there, that's where the ladder ends at the first level. Nice big platform. Over here, another ladder goes up there. And when you get to the top level, there's even a roof. It's a castle in the trees."

"If you say so. I'll just work out the pricing based on the needed materials."

"No need. Thanks for your time," Cooper stood and shook the man's hand.

Connor followed his brother to the door. Once they were outside and out of earshot of the employee they'd just bamboozled, he burst into laughter. "Gotta hand it to you, bro. You sure pulled that one off."

"And with style."

"Okay, with style."

It had been a massive disappointment that the mill wasn't abandoned like the house, but how their expedition ended made up for it.

His phone vibrated in the leg pocket of his cargo pants. Connor pulled it out. It was a text from Mitch.

Worried about N. She freaked out at the boathouse. She's headed back to the house. I'm right behind her.

"Shit. That's from Mitch. He says Nicki freaked out at the boathouse."

"Then we best get back to Kembleford Manor, pronto," said Cooper as he broke into a run.

"I'm fine, Mitch, really. Just startled by what I saw. I don't understand why I'm seeing these things. It's like shadows of the past trying to channel their stories through me if that makes any sense."

"I sent Connor a text and told him what happened."

"Gee, thanks. I'll have both my brothers thinking their sister has gone doo lally, bonkers, ape poop, whatever." Nicole threw her hands in the air and paced in a circle.

"Nick, what happened?" Cooper asked as he rushed to her side.

"You look like you've seen a ghost," said Connor.

"She did see a ghost, guys. Tell them what you saw, Nicki," Mitch urged. "No one will make fun of you or think you're crazy. I've seen your sketches of things you've seen mostly as you've been creating them."

"Okay, but you must promise me you won't laugh or tease me."

Her brothers agreed.

"The boathouse smells like dead fish. Even Mitch had to agree with that."

He nodded.

"As I stood in the doorway, I didn't want to go inside because of the smell; I saw the body of a little girl, ten years old at the most, floating face-down in the water. Next to her body was a china head doll. She wasn't real because she was translucent. I could see the river bottom and the other parts of the boathouse through her and her clothing."

By now, Nicole was shaking. Connor put his arm around her shoulders and started walking her back to the house.

"Did you draw what you saw? Get it on your camera?" Cooper asked. It wasn't that he didn't believe his sister, but he was the kind of person who wanted to see physical evidence of her visions.

"I sketched her. I remember doing that, but I'm not sure if I took a photo. I'll have to check the SD card. Right now, I just want to go home. This place is doing my head in."

"You'll be fine." Mitch stepped closer to Nicole. "Do you want me to see if this town has a Timmie's and get us some coffee?"

"I'm jumpy enough. I don't need a jolt of caffeine to make it worse. Thanks anyway."

Cooper walked ahead of the other three. He didn't know what to make of Nicole's visions. He wondered again about the basement. It seemed too small for a house that size. Unless a portion of it had been closed off, part of the house had no basement. This far north and a house built on grade? It's a wonder it was still standing. He preferred to believe his earlier theory. That was unless there was something more sinister involved behind the blocking. Now he was thinking like his sister. Something he'd read popped into his mind. News or fiction? He couldn't remember, only that after some investigation, body parts preserved in jars of formaldehyde, and an assortment of knives and cleavers had been found in a cellar behind a false wall.

"The only other place we haven't checked yet is the turret between the front windows," Cooper said.

"No idea how to access it. Maybe the families who lived here before closed off entry to it like they did to the one bedroom," Nicole said.

"Well, let's find out."

The four entered the house and slowly reached the top of the stairs.

"Connor, you and Mitch try in that room. Nicki, you're with me. We'll check the other one. There has to be a way in there."

"Nicki and I tried there already. The only door that would lead to it has a solid wall behind it," Mitch said. "Someone filled it in long before we got here."

Not believing Mitch, Cooper walked into the room and opened the door on the wall that adjoined the tower access. A wall. It had been papered to match the rest of the bedroom. He pushed against it, but it didn't budge.

"Mitch was right," Nicole said.

Cooper led the way into the second bedroom. "Access has to be along this wall. Look at this corner just inside the door. It's back far enough the door can open wide, but there's definitely a gap between here and the other bedroom. He tapped on the wall. Solid. Moved forward another three feet and tapped again. Solid. He repeated it again, and the resounding noise was hollow this time.

"Shh, do you hear that?" Nicole asked.

"Hear what?"

"It sounded like someone moving furniture up above us. Scraping chair or table legs being dragged across the floor."

Seeing things. Hearing things. Smelling things. Nicole's reactions to the house covered three of the five senses. The only two missing, and maybe she had experienced them, were touch and taste. Too gross to even think about.

A wardrobe stood along the wall next to where the hollow sound emanated. He opened the door. It was empty, apart from some wire hangers. He pushed on the back. Nothing happened. He ran his hands up and down the back and the sides. Still nothing. Then he repeated his actions on the floor. Something moved under his hand, and the back of the wardrobe opened.

Cooper would have much rather excluded Mitch from the discovery, but it wasn't fair since he and his brother were right there in the room. "Connor, Mitch, I've found the way into the tower."

Nicole stepped through into a small room. "It's like *The Lion, the Witch, and the Wardrobe*, right?"

"Yeah, except this isn't Narnia."

"Come on, guys, let's go," Connor said when he peered through the opening.

"Shouldn't one of us stay here in case the door closes and we're trapped in there?" Mitch asked.

Cooper took a couple of the wire hangers off the rail. "I'll rig the door so it can't close." He wanted to be a part of the discovery. But if Mitch volunteered to stay behind ... So much for that thought; he had already entered. With the hangers hooked together, and bent, Cooper put the hook around the knob on the front door and the loop of the other one around the handle of the adjacent dresser drawer. That looked after the front. He'd grab two or more to keep the rear door ajar.

"Wow, look at this room," Nicole exclaimed. She stood near the base of a spiral staircase and stared up into the void above.

The sound of something heavy being dragged across the floor above her filled the room. "Did you hear that?" she asked.

"No."

That was the consensus of the three men. Only she heard it. This area wasn't scary. She wasn't overcome by the same feeling of profound sadness here that she'd experienced in other parts of the house. Nicole pulled her sketchbook out of her backpack and made a quick drawing. She also took photos with her camera to compare the images later.

"You guys coming?" She started up the spiral staircase and stopped after the third step. The next one had a footprint in the dust. Camera brought to her eye, she photographed the sight before her. The rest of the steps all had the same mark. Men's footwear. Boots, shoes? But not of the current era. The imprint was too heavy for that and too defined. Trainers like they were all wearing left one continuous mark. These were two. The section of the shoe under the ball of the foot and the heel.

Climbing a spiral staircase wasn't easy, but looking where you're walking through your camera's viewfinder made it almost impossible. Still, Nicole didn't want to miss a thing. Finally, she reached the top. The trap door was open, and a railing surrounded the stairs on three sides. A few cobwebs stretched between the rafters, but no creepy crawlies existed.

The same footprints she'd seen on the stairs were up here, as were drag marks from a heavy object. But now, they were accompanied by another set of footprints. These were smaller and looked more like women's than men's. The window was dirty and infested with spider webs, so it wasn't letting in much light. Nicole pulled out her phone and turned on the flashlight. Over on the far side of the room, under the eaves, was what appeared to be an old steamer trunk. She waited for the others before exploring her surroundings any further.

Soon, her brothers and Mitch joined her. Cooper had his headlamp on, so she switched off the light on her phone and returned it to the back pocket of her pants.

"How long do you think it's been since anyone was up here?" she asked.

"Hard to say. The window says quite a while. The dust says something different. Especially with the footprints and drag marks."

"You see them, too? It's not just me?"

"I see them, sis," Connor replied.

After Cooper and Mitch agreed they could see the prints on the floor, Nicole felt better. This time, it wasn't her imagination or some other supernatural phenomenon. Well, it might be that, but this was the first time everyone had seen the same thing.

"I want to see what's in that trunk," she said as she approached its location. "Can I have some light, please, Cooper?"

Although the trunk wasn't locked, the latches were stiff from lack of use. When they finally released, Nicole slowly lifted the lid. Because of the location, it wouldn't open completely, so she had to drag it out from under the sloped ceiling. Once away from the wall, the lid opened entirely.

Fragile tissue paper covered the contents within. Nicole dropped to her knees and carefully removed it. The top layer was bedding. Hand-stitched quilts and knitted and crocheted items. She removed these and sat them on the wrappings. Beneath the blankets were an assortment of items. Silver sugar bowl and tongs, creamer, and a salt cellar with a small spoon. "This stuff is priceless," she exclaimed. The bottoms of the pieces and the backs of the handles were stamped with the initials PS and symbols. She handed one of the pieces to Mitch and then photographed the marks. She'd look it up online from home.

With care, she set the delicate silver pieces on the bedding and returned to the trunk's contents. A long white nightgown came out next. Nicole gasped. It was the nightdress the ghost in the window had worn. The one that was holding what she assumed was a baby.

"You okay, sis?" Connor asked.

"I think so. When I saw the ghost in the room's window that's been sealed off, she … it was wearing this. Hold it up so I can take a picture of it."

Connor did as he was asked. "Does it match the colour of my eyes?" he asked, then laughed.

"It's definitely you," Cooper said.

"Yup, you for sure," replied Mitch.

"Okay, guys, let's be serious. If the ghost wore this, does that mean this trunk is filled with her things?" Nicole asked, folding the garment and placing it aside. An infant's christening gown and crocheted baby blanket came out next. Again, Nicole asked the guys to hold the items so she could photograph them. Other baby items, booties and bonnets were also tucked away, preserved for the next generation to use. Except they were still here. There couldn't have been a next generation. A packet of letters tied in a faded lavender ribbon and another document lay on the bottom.

Nicole pulled the lone sheet of paper out of the trunk and unfolded it. "It's a death certificate."

"Whose?" Mitch asked.

"Just a minute. The writing is hard to read. It looks like the last name is Randall, and the first name is Anna."

"The Christening gown was hers?" Connor asked.

"I don't know yet, but I'm guessing so." She continued to peruse the document. "Okay, the father was Bartholomew Randall here in Pike Falls. The mother was Ophelia Kembleford."

"What's the date?"

"Looks like July 31, 1914."

"Cause?"

Nicole searched the document more closely. "It's hard to read, but it looks like premature birth — stillborn." A tear escaped her eye, and she dashed it away before the guys noticed her crying. "The poor wee thing never had a chance."

"This place is Kembleford Manor, albeit with hotel tacked on the end," Cooper said. "So we know of at least one Kembleford who lived here."

"And died here," Nicole said. "I want to take a picture of this certificate. Maybe I can manipulate the image to get more information from it." She spread it out on the floor and knelt over it with her camera. She took a couple of shots with it, then pulled her phone out of her pocket and took a few more. Surely, between the two devices, she'd come up with a clear image.

After taking the pictures, she folded the certificate and returned it to the trunk. Her hand hovered over the bundle of letters. Did she? That would be theft. Who would know? She would, and so would Mitch and her brothers. Did the letters hold a clue as to the identities of the house's former residents? Maybe some insight into their daily lives? Curiosity got the better of her, and she snatched the package and shoved it into her backpack. Once everything else was returned to the trunk, she latched it up, and her brothers moved it back to its original location.

A profound sadness came over Nicole once more as she gathered her things. As she was about to descend the spiral staircase, a vision appeared. The ghost of the young mother stood barefoot on a chair with a rope secured over the beam and the other end wrapped around her neck. She stepped off the chair and kicked it away. No struggle to save herself. She died with no fight.

Nicole knew she'd never set foot in the house again but was determined to discover its history. This time, she didn't reach for her sketchbook. The ghost of Ophelia Kembleford Randall, if that's who she was, didn't deserve the indignity of having her suicide immortalized on paper.

Chapter Thirteen

Bartholomew strode to his employer's closed office door. He needed to discuss a discrepancy he discovered in the books. He rapped on the door and waited.

"Who's there?"

"Mr. Kembleford. It's Bartholomew Randall. Sir, I wonder if I might have a moment of your time."

"Come in."

The office was tastefully decorated, although not to the same opulence as his study at home. This was a more functional place. Bartholomew walked towards the desk holding the large ledger book.

"Well, what is it?"

"Sir, Mr. Kembleford. I noticed something strange in the financials this morning."

"Oh. Oh really?"

"Yes, sir. May I show you?" He came around the corner of the desk, placed the book on the surface, and pointed to a line. "Here, sir. There's a considerable cash outlay, yet I can't find an invoice to match it. You wouldn't have it in here, would you?"

"Um-um, no. Maybe it was recorded in the wrong ledger. Maybe it was incoming instead of outgoing."

His boss appeared nervous. Why should he? Unless he was involved in something illegal.

"I'll check that, sir. Thank you."

"Off you go now, and let me get back to what I

was doing."

When the door closed behind Bartholomew, Albert Kembleford sighed and sank into his chair. He had almost been caught. He'd have to be more careful in the future. Why did he get tangled up in the weekly poker nights? When he first started playing, he did all right and won quite often. Then things changed, and his luck ran out. He withdrew small amounts from the household account to pay his debts, but when he ended up behind there, he had to borrow from the company. That's all it was. A loan. It would be repaid with interest once his luck changed and he began winning again.

Albert was addicted to gambling. He knew that. But what made it worse was that he couldn't bring himself to tell his wife that he'd lost all their money. That was too much shame for him to bear. No, he'd continue the card games until he won back what he'd lost. Now, he had to keep Bartholomew from discovering his secret. That wouldn't be an easy task. The young man was bright, not to mention his son-in-law.

He have to figure out a way to get out of the predicament he'd gotten himself into. And soon. The annual audit of the mill's books was coming up in a few months.

Chapter Fourteen

MAY 19, 1914

Patience sat at the writing desk in the corner of the living room. Something about her husband had niggled at her from earlier in the year. Maybe even late the previous year. She couldn't put her finger on it, but he was more evasive and not talkative. Before, he talked about the lumber mill, not in great financial detail, but at least interesting anecdotes from the day-to-day operations. Now, she didn't get even that. And then there was the fact he was out many nights during the week until after she retired.

She opened the drawer where she kept her writing paper and selected a sheet, then drew ink from the well into her fountain pen and began to write.

19 May, 1914

Dearest Mother,

I feel guilty bothering you with this, but there's no one else I can talk to about it. Catherine is no longer with us. Now that the children are older, we saw no need to keep a nursery maid in our employ. Matilda is still running a tight ship here, keeping everyone to heel. I hope I said that correctly.

Ophelia is expecting. It's all very exciting. We might need to recall Catherine when the baby arrives, that is, if she'll return to us. Ophelia's husband,

Bartholomew, works with Albert as one of his accounts clerks. That was how they met. They're coming up on being married for three years, but I told you that back then. They live here in the manor house with us. I never thought I would see the day that Ophelia would be married. When she was young, she was more interested in boy things.

James has moved on. He's working on a farm near Grafton, about twelve hours south of where we are here in Pike Falls. He's not given any indication of settling down and taking a wife as yet, but he still could. Maybe he's waiting for the right moment to introduce us to her. That is, if there's a her.

Lavinia is still here, too. She's a shameless flirt, and I've called her to task many times over her behaviour. Especially when Bartholomew is on the receiving end of her flirtations.

But on to the crux of the matter. Albert hasn't been himself since the beginning of the year. I've asked him what's bothering him, and he shuts me out or says nothing is wrong. He won't talk to me about it. I want to know if it has something to do with the lumber mill. He spends more and more evenings away from the house. I don't know where he goes or who he's with. Even if he shut himself away in the study after our evening meal, he was always here before, especially when the children were growing up. I don't know if he's keeping company with another woman. I've not smelled unfamiliar perfume on him or his clothing, so maybe it's just my imagination. Maybe he's drinking in one of the local taverns. I'm afraid I'm losing him, Mother, and I'm helpless to prevent it.

I know tensions are running high with what could be the onset of war. If Albert was preoccupied with that, he'd tell me. I know he would. Forgive me for rambling, mother. It's times like now, I rue the day we sailed from Liverpool.

Love to you and father.
Your loving daughter,

Patience

With the letter to her mother written, she addressed an envelope. Tomorrow, she would walk to the local post office and mail it. This was one of the many nights Albert was out, doing God knew what with God knew who. Patience drained the remaining ink from her pen back into the ink well and screwed the cap back on the writing implement, then put the lid back on the bottle.

She sighed, turned out the lights and went upstairs to her bed.

She wasn't sure when Albert came home, but he was at the table when she came downstairs for breakfast. His eyes were bloodshot, so he'd either been drinking to excess or had not slept. "Good morning, dear," she said when she entered the dining room.

Albert grunted in reply, picked up his cup and drank the last of his coffee. "Goodbye. I must get to the mill. Don't wait supper for me. I shan't be home to eat it."

"What are you hiding from me, Albert?"

"N-nothing." He dabbed his mouth with his napkin and stood. Before he left the room, he walked to Patience's side and kissed her cheek.

Maybe Bartholomew knew what was going on. He should be down for breakfast soon. Her son-in-law was a good worker but didn't put in her husband's long, arduous hours. This morning was the worst she'd seen her husband look after one of his late nights.

Bartholomew and Ophelia entered the dining room together.

"Good morning, Mother," her daughter said.

"Good morning, Mother Kembleford. I take it Mr. Kembleford has already left for the mill?"

"Yes. Speaking of that, do you know why your father-in-law is acting so strangely? Staying out until all hours?"

"N-no," Bartholomew coughed.

He knew. He was in cahoots with Albert. Patience swore she'd get to the bottom of whatever the pair of them were involved in.

Bartholomew wolfed down his breakfast and

70

dashed out. He returned as quickly, gave Ophelia a peck on the cheek and was gone again.

"What has gotten into the men of this family?" Patience asked.

"I'm not sure what you mean, mother. Bartholomew was running late this morning, that's all." Ophelia returned to her bowl of porridge.

"I have to go into Pike Falls this morning. Would you like to come along with me? The fresh air and sunshine might put some colour in your cheeks. You're far too pale. With you in the family way, you must take better care of yourself."

"Yes, Mother. I know. I wouldn't mind a walk."

Lavinia entered the room. "Your sister and I are going into Pike Falls after breakfast. Do you want to join us?" Patience asked.

"No thanks. I've got a Jane Austen on the go, and I when I quit reading last night, it was getting to a really good spot. I want to get back to it."

"Suit yourself."

"Where do you have to go today, Mother?"

"The post office. I have a letter to mail to your granny."

"Did you tell her about me?" Ophelia asked as she pulled her shawl around her shoulders. The sun was bright and warming, but the breeze was cool. She shivered.

"Yes. Are you all right? You're shivering."

"I'm fine, mother. I'm not sure why, but since I became with child, I've been freezing all the time."

"I suppose that's better than being hot and sweating. At least you can always put more clothing on."

Ophelia kicked a stone. It rolled ahead of her about three feet, and when she reached it, she kicked it again. She missed her older brother. They used to play kick about when they were younger. They climbed trees, too. James broke his arm doing the latter when he fell from the branch and landed awkwardly. She'd never broken a bone but had more than her share of scrapes, bumps, cuts, and bruises.

"How is Granny? You don't get a lot of letters from her."

"When she does write, they're short because of her rheumatism, but she says she and Grampy are both fine. But then she would say that so that I don't worry. After all, they are getting up in years."

"Do you ever regret leaving England?" Ophelia rubbed her hands together to warm them.

Her mother hesitated. Did that mean she regrets the move? Ophelia might have been born, same with Lavinia, but if her parents hadn't sailed to Canada, she wouldn't have met and fallen in love with Bartholomew.

Before long, they arrived at the Post Office. "I want to go into Pike's Ladies Wear and look at dresses. Mine are getting tight. I'll soon need some specialty ones. I'll go in there while you're visiting with the postmistress."

The two women parted company. Ophelia strolled up the street to the shop she wanted to visit.

"Mrs. Kembleford, lovely to see you," Post Mistress Brown said as Patience entered the building. "What can I do for you today?"

"The usual. I'm mailing a letter to my mother back in England."

"That's nice. I'll just weigh it for you, and we'll go from there, shall we?"

With the postage calculated, Patience paid the woman, and the stamps were affixed to the envelope.

"Did I see your daughter with you earlier?"

"Yes. Ophelia's off to the dress shop. I'd love to stay and chat with you, but I should get off. Is there any mail for us? I might as well pick it up while I'm here."

"Just your personal mail, or are you collecting the mail for the mill, too?"

"Personal only. Albert wouldn't thank me for getting the business mail."

The postmistress disappeared into the back room and returned with a stack of envelopes. "Here you be. Have a lovely day."

Patience tucked the mail in her handbag and set

off to meet her daughter.

Ophelia browsed the section of empire-waisted gowns. She found two she liked. Both were more formal than everyday attire, but she needed something with less tailoring. Matilda had let out the side seams in her dresses as much as she could, and at the rate the baby was growing, if she didn't get some different styled gowns, she'd have to wear her nightgowns morning, noon and night. While they were comfortable, they weren't fashionable or suitable for anyone other than her husband to see her wearing.

"Mother, you finished quickly. I wasn't expecting to see you so soon."

"I was the only customer, so there was no queue ahead of me."

"What do you think of these two gowns?" Ophelia held up a navy blue chiffon one in her left hand and a cardinal red satin one in her right. Both gowns had high necklines and long sleeves with buttoned cuffs at the wrists. The buttons were rhinestones. The same embellishment was on the front from the collar to the high waist.

"They're both lovely. And the style, too. Suitable for a mother-to-be in the family way."

"I'm going to get both of them. I hope they won't be too hard for Matilda to launder."

"Perhaps you should go for a more practical fabric like linen or cotton."

"I looked at some in those fabrics, but they didn't appeal to me. They were so drab by comparison." Ophelia held each gown in turn in front of her and stood before the full-length mirror. These were perfect. They were so her. She had plenty of cotton and linen clothing at home and even wool items for the cooler months. Now that her mind was definitely made up, she walked both garments to the counter. "I'll take them both."

The store clerk removed the dresses from their hangers, carefully folded them, and wrapped them in tissue paper before placing them in a box. As she worked, she wrote out the receipt. When the two articles of clothing were boxed up, she tied it with string.

Ophelia paid the woman. They cost her double her regular clothing allowance, but she was sure Bartholomew wouldn't be angry once he saw her in them.

When they arrived back at the manor, Patience removed the mail from her handbag and walked it into Albert's study. She leafed through it, hoping for a letter from James or her mother, but there was none. How long had it been since she'd heard from her son? It had to be at least six months. She had replied to his last letter, hadn't she? She must have. That was the first thing she did after she read his letters. Had he moved and not sent her his new address? Maybe tomorrow would bring news from him.

Patience left the mail on the desk and closed the door behind her. Anything that she left there were things Albert dealt with. She rang the bell to summon Matilda when she reached the living room. The young maid scurried into the room.

"Yes, Mrs. Kembleford?"

"Is there any lemonade left?"

"Yes, ma'am. Would you like me to get you a glass?"

"Yes, please."

The front doorbell rang. With Matilda off getting her some refreshments, Patience answered the door herself. The postmistress stood outside.

"I'm very sorry to bother you, Mrs. Kembleford, but I thought you would like this letter. It had fallen behind the mail slots, and I didn't see it until I bent down to pick something else up. It's from your son, I think."

Patience took the envelope from the woman. It looked like her son's handwriting. She turned it over, searching for a return address, but there was none. She always put one on her letters to her mother in England, as did she when she replied. "Thank you very much for bringing this to me. Would you like to stay for a glass of lemonade? Matilda has gone to get me one."

"No, thank you. Mrs. Kembleford. I must be getting back. I can't leave my mister too long. He's not been well of late."

"Sorry to hear that. In that case, you best be off. Thank you again for delivering this letter."

Patience closed the door and returned to the living room. She arrived just as Matilda was bringing her the cool drink. "I'll have it at my writing desk, please."

The Maid of All Work placed the glass where she was asked and scurried out of the room. Mrs. Kembleford sat down. She searched for her letter opener. It was shaped like a dagger and was sharp, too. She tore open the envelope and let it fall to the floor as she unfolded the paper. It was from James.

April 30, 1914

Dear Mother,

I'm sorry I've been lax in sending you letters. This is my first chance to write to you in a long time. I've been busy with work on the farm. I wasn't sure how I would take to farm work, but I am enjoying it immensely. The family I'm working for are kind to me and pay me well in my position as farm hand. Farm work doesn't stop just because there is snow on the ground. The animals still need feeding, stalls need cleaning, and the cows need milking twice daily. The first one gets done before we get to have breakfast.

And what breakfasts they are! An enormous bowl of porridge followed by bacon, eggs, toast, and more. Lunches are usually soup and sandwiches followed by pie for dessert. And the suppers are every bit as big as the breakfasts. Meat, potatoes, vegetables, homemade bread and butter, cheese, dessert. Sometimes it's pie and other times, it's cake. Mrs. O'Connor, the farmer's wife, makes the most delicious chocolate cake. You would love it. They also have a daughter, Marie. She's about my age and helps her mother with the women's work — cooking, cleaning, washing, gathering the eggs, feeding the chickens, and so on.

There's about three feet of snow on the ground now. Mr. O'Connor is afraid we won't be able to get out to work the fields and plant the crops until after King George V Day on June 3. Do you have much snow up north?

The farmer and his wife are about yours and Father's age. Who knows, when they decide the farm is too much for them, I might buy it.

I hope you are all well up in Pike Falls. Are Ophelia and Lavinia still scrapping like a pair of alley cats? Oh, I remember some doozies they had.

Please write to me soon. Even though I don't always have time to answer your letters, I appreciate you sending them and keeping me informed of the family news here and abroad.

Your son,

James

It wasn't a long letter, but she'd heard from him. That was the main thing. He was doing well and, by all accounts, happy working on the O'Connor farm. The hard work would do him good. James wasn't cut out to run a company or work in an office. He liked to get his hands dirty. He liked hard physical work. This was the first time he'd mentioned the family had a daughter about his age. Perhaps he might be thinking about courting this girl with a mind to marrying her?

She should write back to him immediately but decided to wait until she'd shown his letter to her husband. He might have something he'd like to add when she responded.

Chapter Fifteen

Bartholomew Randall patted his pockets for his house key. He shoved his hands into his trouser pockets, but still nothing. He cranked the doorbell. When no one came immediately to answer it, he rang again, then pounded on the leaded glass window. Footsteps scurried towards him, becoming louder as the person drew nearer.

Matilda, the Kembleford's Maid of All Work, opened the door. "Mr. Randall, what has you in such a state?

"Is Mr. Kembleford here?" He asked, panting to catch his breath.

"The mister isn't here. Isn't he at the mill?"

"No, I just came from there. What about Mother Kembleford? Ophelia? Even Lavinia?"

"The missus and her daughters are in the sitting room. Why didn't you use your key?"

"I don't have it with me." Bartholomew pushed by the young girl and raced to the second door on the left.

"Why, Bartholomew, what has you so vexed?" Ophelia, the young man's wife, asked as she rose from the sofa.

"It's terrible. Just terrible. Mrs. Kembleford, ma'am, the Bailiff, and the police are at the mill. The Bailiff is there to lock the mill down, and the policeman is going to arrest your husband. I might even be arrested. It's a catastrophe."

Bartholomew finally stopped talking and took a deep breath. A loud bang rang out from somewhere inside the manor house. It sounded much like a heavy object falling onto a wooden floor.

"My goodness, what in heaven's name was that?" Mrs Kembleford asked.

"I don't know, but it sounded like it came from Father's study," said Ophelia, dropping her knitting project on the couch.

The entrance to the room was across the foyer and to the right at the head of a long, narrow corridor. Bartholomew led the women to his employer's study. He turned the knob and pushed, but the door held. He knelt down and peered through the keyhole. The skeleton key was in the lock from the other side. "Quick, a sheet of paper and something long and thin I can poke through the hole. We have to get in there."

Ophelia dashed to the sitting room and returned with a sheet of her mother's finest writing vellum and one of the knitting needles she'd been using when Bartholomew arrived. "Will these work?"

He snatched the objects from her and slid the sheet of paper under the door below the knob, then stuck the pointed end of the wooden stick through the keyhole and prodded and pushed until the key was successfully pushed out of the lock and dropped with a soft thud to the floor. His actions would have been for naught if the gap under the door wasn't wide enough. Bartholomew took a deep breath and began to slide the paper towards him. Success! The key rested on the paper, and there was enough space to fit through the opening.

"Where did you learn how to do that?" Ophelia asked.

Bartholomew smiled but remained silent. He put the key in the lock and turned it until the bolt retracted with a loud click. He pushed the door open, closed it quickly and turned to the women crowded behind him. "You don't want to go in there."

"Nonsense," Mrs. Kembleford said. She pushed past the man and pushed her way into the room, followed by her daughters. She clutched her chest and went limp. Bartholomew sprang into action and stopped the woman from hitting the floor when she fainted. "Close the door," he said to Ophelia, "and you both come and help me look after your mother." He carried her to the sofa in the sitting room.

His earlier panic vanished as he took control of the situation. "Lavinia, you go to the mill. Bring the policeman who's there back with you." The constable was the last person he wanted to see, but he'd do it, given the circumstances. When Bartholomew discovered the embezzling, he cooked the mill's books to cover it up. He was as guilty as his employer, who was also his father-in-law. The secret had to remain buried.

She glared at him.

"Go. Now," Bartholomew shouted. "Ophelia, is your mother prone to fainting? If so, do you keep smelling salts in the house?"

"I-I've never seen her faint before. Maybe Matilda has some."

"Go. Quickly."

Bartholomew settled his mother-in-law on the sofa and patted the back of her hand to rouse her, but his attempts were in vain. Ophelia returned a short time later with the ammonium carbonate and handed the small vial over. He removed the bottle's stopper and waved it under Mrs. Kembleford's nose. The pungent smell brought her around. Once she was awake, he put the top back on the bottle.

At that moment, a severe cramp hit Ophelia's abdomen. She wrapped her hands around her middle as she doubled over. She couldn't be in labour, could she? It was way too soon. By hers and her doctors calculations, she was only about six months along. "Ow," she cried. "I'm in pain."

"What is it, love?"

Ophelia raised her head and looked at her husband. "I think the baby is coming."

The colour drained from Bartholomew's face. "Now?"

"Yes."

"What do you want me to do?"

"I need the doctor or the midwife. Quickly!" Another pain shot through her. She grabbed Bartholomew's hand and squeezed. Hard.

He couldn't leave the house, not with his mother-in-law in no fit state to look after her daughter. He had already sent Lavinia to the mill. What was he going to do? "Let's get you upstairs and into bed. You'll be more comfortable there."

She nodded.

Bartholomew half walked, and half carried his wife up the stairs to their bedroom, where he settled her on their four-poster bed. Lavinia shouldn't be too much longer. Not if she went with the speed, he'd hoped she would. The day started out all right, but it sure took a turn for the worse with the arrival of the Bailiff and police at the mill. He didn't want the business closed and those men thrown out of work. Most of them were young enough that if Canada got involved in the impending war in Europe, they could serve in the army. Small consolation. Stay here, be out of work for who knows how long, or go overseas and fight and maybe never return.

No doubt, there was a warrant for his arrest in the offing. He knew what he'd done was wrong but had only done it to protect his father-in-law. That didn't do any good, either. Did the man know that this was happening today, and that's why he returned home and subsequently killed himself? He didn't know Albert even owned a gun.

Men's voices downstairs drifted up the staircase. Bartholomew ensured his wife was comfortable and went downstairs. He hadn't expected the Bailiff to accompany the police, but they were both there.

"Lavinia, your sister needs the doctor, or at the very least, the midwife. Would you please go fetch one of them back here? Fast as you can. Ophelia thinks she's having the baby."

"But it's too early."

"I know that, but we need to be prepared. Please go."

"Would you excuse me, gentlemen? I must return to my wife."

"Yes. Young Miss Kembleford needed us here immediately. Me more than the Bailiff," the policeman said.

"I almost forgot about that." Like a dead body with half his head blown off was something he'd be likely to forget in his lifetime. "When we discovered Mr. Kembleford's death, I closed the door right away. We didn't go into the room."

"And which one is it?"

"This one." He escorted the constable to the door.

Ophelia's scream from upstairs echoed in the enclosed space.

"I really must go." Bartholomew turned and took the stairs two at a time to return to his wife's side.

"It hurts so bad, Bartholomew," Ophelia said when he returned.

"You'll be fine. Maybe it's not the baby at all. Maybe it's something you ate earlier today."

Men, they didn't have a clue when it came to babies and labour and anything that related to being a woman.

"The police are here dealing with your father's suicide. I've sent Lavinia to get the doctor if he's not out on a call somewhere, and if he is, then she's to track down the midwife and bring her back as fast as she can."

Ophelia rolled onto her side and drew her knees towards her chest. At least as far as she could, given her pregnant state. The pains were too close together. Didn't they start farther apart and then get closer? She stared at the mantle clock on the fireplace. It was difficult to see through her tear-filled eyes.

"We don't even have any names picked out yet," she said.

"James," Bartholomew said. "That's a fine name for a son." He wiped his hands down his thighs.

"And what if it's not a boy?" Ophelia shifted positions and propped herself up on her elbows.

"Anna. There it's settled."

Bartholomew stood again and paced back and forth by the foot of the bed.

"Will you please sit down? I'm getting dizzy watching you?"

Where was Lavinia with either the doctor or the midwife? She should have been back by now. Bartholomew glanced at Ophelia lying on the bed. She was calm at the moment. How long it would last, he had no idea. He was the youngest of six, so by the time he came along, his mother's child-bearing years were over. And his siblings were all boys. Not a James in the lot. He liked that name. His brother-in-law was a James. It was a man's name. Not like the moniker he was stuck with. Who named their son Bartholomew? His mother for one. Even a bastardized version of the name, Bart, wasn't any better. Five older brothers and they all got decent names. Normal names. William, John, Robert, Charles, and Richard. Whatever influenced his mother's decision when he was born, he wished it would have stayed away.

Lavinia arrived with the midwife who promptly sent him out of the room. "We don't need any men in here when baby is ready to come. Off you go."

"But ..."

"Scoot," she said, making shooing gestures with her hands.

Bartholomew paused in the doorway. As he did, Ophelia let out a scream then mumbled something he didn't quite catch. Something about hating him. At least that's what it sounded like.

Bartholomew grudgingly left the bedroom and walked to the room set up as the nursery. Catherine Pritchard, the Nursery Maid, had scrubbed the room from floor to ceiling and laundered everything in scalding hot water a few days ago. Did she see something in Ophelia he had missed? Maybe, being employed in that position for various families over the years, she could pick up on the tiniest nuances in a woman with child that told her the birth was imminent.

He stood in the middle of the room. A rocking chair in one corner by the window. The cradle that Ophelia and Lavinia slept in as infants was nearer the door, and a larger bed with high sides and wooden rails was against the wall next to the room's entrance. A four-drawer chest rounded out the furnishings. It was a comfortable room with only the basics. A baby didn't need much. Certainly not as much as an older child or an adult.

Another scream from his and Ophelia's bedroom. He couldn't be in there. The midwife kicked him out. Downstairs was out of the question, too. The policeman and the Bailiff were down there. With his wife being in the process of giving birth, maybe they would at least wait until after the blessed event to arrest him.

"Give us one more big push, Mrs. Randall. I can see baby's head."

Ophelia complied. "I'm exhausted. Can I rest a minute?" She flopped back onto the bed and wiped her sweaty forehead with the sleeve of her nightgown. She didn't remember the midwife getting her out of her day gown and into it. Same with the extra blankets and flannels under her. Did you have lapses in memory when you gave birth?

"And another. We're almost there."

She bore down again. This time the baby slithered out. "Is it a boy or a girl?" Ophelia tried to lean forward so she could see better. "How come it's not crying? Shouldn't it be crying?" She started to panic. What was wrong with her child?

The midwife rubbed the baby's back and chest with one of the pieces of flannel.

"What are you doing?"

"Sometimes, baby needs a bit more stimulation to start breathing on her own."

"It's a girl?"

"Yes. A beautiful, baby girl. Do you have a name

picked out for her yet?"

"Anna."

"That's a beautiful name." The midwife stopped what she was doing and massaged Ophelia's abdomen. "We need to deliver the placenta," the woman said matter-of-factly. No emotion in her voice like before when she was telling Ophelia to push.

"What's wrong with my baby? Is she ...?"

"I'm afraid so. We'll need to contact the local registrar and get the death registered."

Ophelia burst into tears. It couldn't be. First her father and now her daughter? "Can I hold her, please? I want my husband."

The midwife wrapped the body in a blanket and placed it on Ophelia's chest. She unwrapped the bundle. Ten fingers, ten toes, button nose and heart-shaped mouth. Perfect, except she was dead.

Bartholomew returned to their bedroom. Ophelia's tears told him what happened. Words weren't required. He sat on the bed beside her, put an arm around her shoulders, and pulled the blanket back away from the baby's face.

"Anna. She never took a breath. She was dead when I delivered her," Ophelia sobbed.

"We're young. There will be plenty of time for more children."

If looks could kill, then the glare he received from his distraught wife would have dropped him in his tracks. What did he say that was so wrong? They were young. Healthy adults. Unless something terrible was wrong with Ophelia, she could get with child again. This event would have to be registered, but surely it could wait a day or two.

"Your mother should be told, but I think she's too fragile at the moment." He tried to be understanding and sympathetic but his heart was broken, as well. It wasn't just Ophelia who lost a child. He did, too. While he might not have carried her or given birth to her, he lost her.

"I think the midwife was notifying the registrar. I

don't know if we'll have to go to him or if he'll bring the paperwork to us. I hope it's the latter because I don't want to go anywhere."

"We'll deal with it when it happens. If someone has to go to him, then I'll do it. You can stay home. We'll also have to contact the undertaker and make arrangements for her funeral and burial." Bartholomew was trying to be practical. These were things that needed to be done. With the probability of him being arrested looming, the matters had to be attended to quickly. If he concentrated on that, Ophelia could grieve.

"Help me up, please, Bartholomew. I want to take Anna into the nursery.

"Are you sure you should be out of bed? You just had a baby."

"Don't patronize me. I'm not in the mood. I want to take Anna into the nursery and you're going to help me out of this bed."

Ophelia stood in the window of the nursery. The day had turned grey and miserable. Of course it did. A black cloud of doom hovered over Kembleford Manor. Nothing would ever be the same again. She sat in the rocking chair and began to rock slowly and sang a lullaby from her childhood. Normal things for a mother. But nothing would be normal for this mother, or her own mother ever again. July 31 was a day that would blight the calendar for years to come.

Why had her father shot himself in the head? What did Bartholomew know that she didn't, if anything? She had so many questions and no answers. She doubted if her mother even knew what had possessed him to do such a thing. Death was permanent. It wasn't like going to sleep one day and waking up the next. You didn't wake up from death. Death took away all your hurt — permanently.

"Bartholomew Randall," a loud male voice called from below. "I need you to come downstairs."

"What is it?" He turned to his wife and said, "Since I found your father's body, they likely need to speak with me. I'll only be a minute." He leaned down and kissed her forehead.

Bartholomew found the policeman and the Bailiff in the living room along with his mother-in-law and Lavinia. Maybe she gave her mother the sad news about Ophelia's baby.

"Mr. Randall, we've looked at the books you keep for the Kembleford Lumber Mill. They show a business in an excellent financial position. But the company's bank account tells a completely different story. And so does Mr. Kembleford's personal bank account. I put it to you that you knew he was embezzling the company's money and depositing it into his personal coffers. And there were large withdrawals from them as well."

Bartholomew swallowed hard. His forehead became damp. He had to hold it together. He couldn't crack. Not now. Not after looking after things so carefully.

"This letter from the bank found on Mr. Kembleford's desk says it all. FORECLOSURE. When the company money ran out, the bank foreclosed on the lumber mill, the house everything. Now, do you have anything to say?"

He cast his eyes towards the floor and shook his head.

"Bartholomew Randall, I'm arresting you on the charge of falsifying records, fraud, and I'm sure as the investigation continues, there will be more charges added to the list." The policeman handcuffed his hands behind his back and led him out the front door.

Out on the gravel driveway, he looked up at the nursery window. Ophelia stood there with their dead daughter, Anna, in her arms. "I'm so sorry," he said, knowing she couldn't hear him.

Chapter Sixteen

OCTOBER 15, 2022

It was almost midnight when Cooper pulled into the apartment complex's parking lot. "Wake up, bro. We're home." He nudged Connor's shoulder.

He stretched when he climbed out of the driver's seat. As he was about to lock the car, he noticed Nicole's sketchbook in the footwell leaning against the back of the front passenger seat. Did he bring it into the apartment? Leave it there and let her know she'd left it behind? Ultimately, he reached into the vehicle and picked it up, pushed the button on the key fob, and locked the SUV.

Connor was halfway up the walk to the security door when he caught up with him.

"What's that you've got?" Connor asked.

"Nicki's sketchbook. She must have left it when we dropped her off. I'll text her and let her know I have it here."

"She sure wasn't herself when we were exploring that old place. It really got to her. I've never seen her so freaked out."

His brother had a point. The three siblings had explored many abandoned properties, and she never reacted as she did at Kembleford Manor. Some of the places they'd been through were even older than today's destination, so it wasn't just the age of the house that caused her reaction.

Once inside the apartment, Cooper laid the book

on the coffee table.

"I'm going to have a beer before I head to bed. You want one?" Cooper asked.

When he got the response, he took two cans of local craft beer out of the fridge. "On the counter," he said before pulling the ring tab on his drink.

Cooper plopped onto the couch. The long drive had been tiring, even though they stopped for supper on the road. Not only did that help break up the trip, but they were hungry. He should be going to bed rather than sitting up later, but the need to unwind first won out. He pulled out his cell phone and typed a quick message.

U left your sketchbook behind.

Connor picked up the TV remote as he sat in the armchair that matched the sofa. "Texting Nicki?"

"Yes."

Three bouncing dots on the phone's screen indicated someone was composing an incoming message.

"Still not sure what to make of Mitch being there at the same as us. You say you didn't tell him, and Nicki swears she didn't. I sure as hell didn't."

"It worked out okay in the end. I mean, he looked after Nicki — well, not looked after, but stayed with her so she wasn't alone."

"Yeah, there is that."

Cooper's phone pinged.

Thanks. Afraid I lost it. Will swing by tomorrow for it.

The closed sketchbook on the coffee table beckoned Cooper. Nicole's sketches she'd made at Kembleford Manor. At first, he resisted the urge to open the book and look at them. After all, they weren't his. But, maybe if he saw what she'd seen, he could work out why the house had affected her the way it did. He leaned forward, then sat back. No. He wouldn't look. It ranked up there with reading her diary, not that he ever knew if she had one.

Finally, he succumbed to the temptation. He flipped through the other sketches in the book. Closeups of the ceiling medallions in the formal living and dining rooms, a misty image of some undetermined thing obscured the corridor that led to the main entrance. His sister's rendering of the scene on the stairs explained why she was so rattled after the experience. He quickly closed the book and returned it to the coffee table. What did she say the name of the poem was? He remembered the first line. *Yesterday, upon the stair,* so he opened the browser on his phone and typed it in. The first entry that came up was Wikipedia, and the entire poem was there.

> *Yesterday, upon the stair,*
> *I met a man who wasn't there*
> *He wasn't there again today*
> *I wish, I wish he'd go away...*
>
> *When I came home last night at three*
> *The man was waiting there for me*
> *But when I looked around the hall*
> *I couldn't see him there at all!*
> *Go away, go away, don't you come back any more!*
> *Go away, go away, and please don't slam the door... (slam!)*
>
> *Last night I saw upon the stair*
> *A little man who wasn't there*
> *He wasn't there again today*
> *Oh, how I wish he'd go away...*

Cooper was the only one who entered the cellar, and that was only because he had to go in through a window and find his way up the stairs to let the others in. It was creepy. Cobwebs everywhere. Dirt floor and rough stone walls. Stank of mould. But that wasn't surprising. The place had been locked up for years, and the foundation hadn't had any waterproofing treatment. In the late 1800s and early 1900s, that wasn't a priority, unlike today, when building codes state that basement walls must be sealed on the exterior. There was another odour, too. Sour. Decomp? Had an animal come in through the broken window and died down there because it couldn't get out?

There was something else in the cellar that niggled him since his foray through it to the steps. It didn't look as large as the rest of the house. Not even close. The majority of the building might have had nothing below it, and this portion only did because they needed a place to dump the coal for the furnace. The old coal furnaces were huge, hulking things and would have occupied most of the available space. There was nothing besides the divider where the coal chute once was. Not a damn thing. Except for the stairs. And cobwebs. The only way to find out for sure was to return to Kembleford Manor and search the basement. He wasn't sure if his curiosity was strong enough to warrant another trip.

Nicole had a restless night. First, she was worried that she'd lost her sketchbook. Second, she was anxious to compare the images on her camera's SD card to the ones in the book. Since she couldn't do any of that, Nicki had started going through the boxes of papers passed on to her by her father.

She'd only made it through one box. Some of what was saved had to have been passed down to her mother and now had found its way into her possession. A copy of Life Magazine from November 1963 — the feature article on the assassination of President Kennedy. That happened the year before her mother was born. It had to have been her grandmother had saved it for future generations. Numerous newspaper clippings regarding the man's death. Another magazine covered the death of Robert Kennedy. More clippings inside the covers. And lastly, the same on Martin Luther King. It was all American historical events. Was there nothing Canadian in here? She rooted around and came up with a Canadian centennial one-dollar bill with 1867-1967 replacing the usual serial number., a complete set of centennial coins, from a penny to a silver dollar. And a commemorative coin that looked like it might have been cast in brass. Her mother would have been three that year. Too young to remember. Too late to ask her.

Damn. Why didn't she talk to her mother and father about their parents and grandparents? Who they were? What did they do? Why didn't they visit more often? Why didn't her parents take Cooper, Connor and her to see them? At least she could still talk to her father and vowed to do it before any more time was wasted. Having seen these documents when her mother was still alive would have been helpful. Then, the opportunity to ask questions would have been there. But it was too late to worry about that now. Her mother's cancer came back with a vengeance in 2019. And in her weakened state, despite receiving the initial dose of the vaccine, she contracted Covid. If not for that, her mother might have survived to fight another day, but it wasn't to be. Masks were a fashion statement in 2020. Her mother only went to the hospital for her chemo treatments. She had to have picked it up there. Or, her father, the only other person she had contact with, picked it up and acted as a carrier and infected the woman. That didn't make sense either because he worked from home. He didn't shop at the grocery store. Ordered the groceries online and used click and collect. He always wore a mask when waiting for the foodstuffs to be brought to the car. It was all water under the bridge now.

The letters. The packet of letters she shoved into her backpack. She could at least read them. Nicole returned the magazines and other tidbits to the box and dumped her rucksack contents onto the floor beside her — pencils, erasers, another sketchbook which had yet to be used, among other things. The packet tied with the discoloured lavender ribbon lay in the middle of the detritus.

Nicole's fingers trembled as she picked up the bundle and untied the bow. The writing was faded on the top envelope and a stamp she'd never seen before. With great care, she removed the contents and laid them flat to read. It was written with a dip pen. She recognized the telltale fading of the ink before the nib was dipped again. She had used one when she did calligraphy at college.

2 December, 1891

Dearest Patience,

This letter is in reply to your letters of 27 September and 1 October. I've only just received them. If only you lived closer or in a major city. The post might move at a quicker pace if that were the case. But it is what it is.

The ship you sailed on sounds very grand, indeed. I'm pleased to know your passage across the ocean was safe and that you're settling into your new home.

Your father is fine. He's had a bountiful season in the garden. I'm pleased he has that to keep him occupied. I've taken to applying goose grease infused with camphor to my hands for my rheumatism. I do it at night when I won't be plunging them in water on a regular basis. I can't embroider anymore. My hands, and well, my eyes, too, aren't up to the task. Your father says I need glasses, but I can manage all the other household chores quite nicely without them.

I'll close now, my dear. You mentioned snow in one of your letters. Has it fallen yet? Christmas will soon be upon us, so I wish you well in your new home with your husband and your son, our grandson.

Love to all.

Your loving mother

It was a letter to one of the earlier occupants of the house from her mother, presumably written in response to the two Patience had written after she and her family arrived in Canada. Would she be lucky enough to find travel documents in one of the other boxes her father gave her? Nicole returned this one to its envelope, placed it face-down on the floor and picked up the next one.

The same handwriting and stamp adorned this one as well. It must be another letter from Patience's mother. The old woman probably didn't write too many letters because of the painful hands she mentioned in the first letter. That also explained how short the letters were.

8 February, 1893

Dearest Patience,

A girl! A granddaughter for your father and me. How lovely. I'm delighted you named the wee one after my mother. She would be thrilled to know that. I'm sorry my letters are so sporadic. It hurts my hands to hold the pen for extended periods of time. I try to keep snippets of events recorded so I can pass stories of them on to you. Unfortunately, I can't always lay my hands on them when I'm ready and able to write. I told you before about the goose grease and camphor. I'm still applying it liberally to my hands every night. Your father complains about the smell.

I'm pleased you were able to hire a Maid of All Work. She must be a great help to you. A Nursery Maid, too? You are becoming quite the lady of the manor. Your description of your house sounds so very elegant. I've read your letters to your father, and he's pictured it in his mind's eye. I could tell that because he got that thoughtful look on his face when I read him the house description.

He's almost popped his buttons with pride, knowing he has a new granddaughter. He's been telling everyone he meets in the village about her, although other than your brief description, there isn't much else to tell.

Do keep us in your thoughts.

Your loving mother

These glimpses of past lives fascinated Nicole. Obviously, the family was well off if they could afford to buy a lumber mill and the house, not to mention, hire two maids. She and her brothers pooled their resources and got a cleaning lady to come in when their mother underwent cancer treatments. Their father did okay but didn't keep it up to their mother's standards.

Nicole got up from the floor. Her foot had gone to sleep from the way she sat on it, and now pins and needles plagued her. She wanted to continue reading the letters but until she got the feeling back in her extremity, she couldn't.

She hobbled out to the galley kitchen and poured herself a glass of cold water from the Brita jug in the fridge. It was refreshing. After pacing around the apartment, she managed to relieve the numbness. That would teach her to sit cross-legged for so long. When she went back to read more of the letters, she'd lean against the couch with her legs outstretched in front of her.

25 February, 1894

Dearest Patience,

Since we received word of Ophelia's birth last year, your father has been given to celebrating to excess. Had we known of Lavinia's birth on the day, he would have been round to the pub wetting the baby's head. As it was, he still went out and bought drinks for all his friends.

I remember the New Year's Eves you speak of. There were many, some before you were old enough to sneak out of your room, and more after you and Albert were wed and set up your own home.

Another baby and another girl! And on the last day of the year. Your father was thrilled when I told him of the birth of yet another granddaughter. I can't think of a better way to start the year than with a new baby in the house. I'm pleased Matilda is keeping you to task and that you have a Nursery Maid, too.

With three small children, on your own, and with that large house ... I assume it's large since you refer to it as a manor house, you need the extra help.

I trust things are still going well for Albert and his lumber mill. You must be so proud. The other children,

*they're well? Lavinia is a lovely name for a little girl. I
don't recall any girls with that name in my family, but
then, I didn't know my grandparents. They died before I
was born. Perhaps there was a Lavinia on your
husband's side?*

Nicole paused and picked up the envelope again. She
tried to read the postmark to find out exactly where
Patience's parents lived, but it was too faded. On the
other ones, too. She went back to the letter.

*Your description of the snow outside your window
sounds lovely. I can't remember when we've had that
much snow here. I think when I was a girl we had one
really bad winter.*

    *Ophelia is quite the character. Imagine giving her
older brother a black eye. My, my.*

    *My hands are starting to hurt, so I must stop now
as I don't recall any other news I could pass on. As
always, I send you mine and your father's love.*

    Keep your father and I in your thoughts.

Your loving mother

The return addresses on the envelopes she'd looked at
so far were faded, but when she picked up the next one,
she could read some of it. There was no name, but a
house name, street, city and county. Butternut Cottage,
Union Street, Market Rasen, Lincolnshire. She could
look that up on Google Maps.

    Despite the late hour, Nicole carried on with the
letters from Patience's mother. The next one in the stack
was dated mid-July 1914. Were they out of order? The
first ones she read followed in logical order. Did Patience
and her mother have a falling out and only recently
reconciled? Or were there letters some place else? This
was only a few of them. That was a twenty-year gap. A
lot could happen in that length of time. Hopefully, she'd
unearth more when she went through the boxes. And
there were a lot of them.

17 July, 1914

Dearest Patience,

> *Another baby in the house, how exciting! And a first grandchild for you. When is the little one expected?*
> *Yes, I remember you telling me of Ophelia's and Bartholomew's marriage. A baby will be just the thing to make her into a proper lady, if her marriage hasn't already.*
> *I'm pleased James is enjoying his job as a farm labourer. It's too bad he had to go so far from you to obtain employment. Surely, there are farms nearer to Pike Falls? That's such a long distance from you.*
> *Oh dear, Lavinia. You're going to have to keep a tighter rein on that girl or she'll cause a scandal otherwise. One of these days her flirtations will go too far and she'll end up in the family way without the benefit of clergy. That would be terrible for your social status as lady of the manor.*
> *I'm sorry I can't tell you what to do about Albert. It's quite possible that he's working harder now that there is going to be a new baby in the house. He never seemed to be the type who would take up with someone else.*
> *You're right about tensions being high because of the war. But not because of what's going on in Europe. Britain is worried more about the threat of a civil war in Ireland. We've seen the papers and know what's happening in the world. The only blessing, such as it is, is your father passed away earlier this year. 1 March to be exact. I tried to write to tell you, but every time I sat down and thought about it, I was reduced to tears. We were together for so long. I miss him terribly.*
> *Please keep me in your thoughts.*

Your loving mother

How tragic. Patience's father died and she didn't find out about it for three and a half months at least. Nicole didn't know if she could carry on reading these letters tonight. The huge clock on her wall read two-thirty. She was wide awake and would only toss and turn if she went to bed. There was only one more letter from this bundle. Once she had read it, she'd wrap them all up again in the ribbon and put them on top of the next box she'd go through.

Was this Patience woman's married name Kembleford? Or was she someone from before the home was named Kembleford Manor? It was possible.

21 September, 1914

My dearest Patience,

My heart breaks for you and Ophelia on your losses. How tragic. I hope you'll both find the strength to get through this. I hope James was able to come home and spend time with you after such a terrible sequence of events. Albert embezzling money from his company? Bartholomew arrested for doctoring the books to hide the misdeeds? Oh my giddy aunt, I can't believe it.

I'm shocked that Lavinia isn't being more supportive in your time of need. That girl needs to pull up her socks and help you both in these troubling times. If I were there, I'd give her a stern talking to.

I do hope the bank shows you some compassion and lets you stay on for a time. This is such a mess. My words of compassion don't seem to be very so. I'm hurt that you both lost your husbands, but with luck Bartholomew won't be too long in jail and he can come back to care for Ophelia. She'll need his support. Stillbirths are terrible. And with this one coming so early, maybe it's a blessing in disguise. The poor child might have had all manner of afflictions and been a burden to her mother. No, as painful as it is for Ophelia, I think this is for the best. She's young and strong and there will be other babies. It was likely her father's greed and doing what he did that caused it. I'm disgusted he took such a cowardly way out by taking his own life.

My letter probably isn't helping you in your grief, but I had to get the words off my chest.

Remember me in your thoughts.

Your loving mother

One minute she's grieving along with Patience and Ophelia and the next she turns on them and tells it like it is. Wow.

Chapter Seventeen

Walter woke refreshed. If there had been any further incidents during the night, Mary had dealt with them quickly before his sleep was disturbed. He threw back the covers and climbed out of bed. At least today, he didn't have to wear a suit. A white cotton short-sleeved shirt and pleated beige trousers were laid out for him. His wife must have done that before they retired the previous evening, but he hadn't noticed.

He glanced towards Grace's room when he turned for the stairs. The door was pulled to but not latched. On his descent, the aroma of freshly brewed coffee and frying bacon wafted up to greet him.

"How's Daddy's little angel this morning?" He leaned down and kissed the top of his daughter's head. The child must have woken up and come down with her mother. Her china doll was in a small high chair beside her.

There was a time when he didn't think he'd ever be a father, so he showered Grace with more attention and affection than needed. Hers was a difficult birth, and he almost lost both her and Mary as a result. But they survived, for which he was grateful.

Mary placed a plate of bacon and eggs in front of him. The coffee pot sat on a trivet in the middle of the table, and he poured himself a large mug.

"Daddy, when people come and stay here, do we

have to feed them?"

His daughter's blue eyes sparkled.

"Yes. Breakfast, at least."

"Will they eat in the kitchen with us?"

It was a huge family kitchen. It would be interesting to visit with the hotel's guests over meals. That was another thing he'd forgotten. A guest-book. That way, they could look back and see how far people had travelled to come stay with them.

Mary placed a package beside him, wrapped in plain brown paper and tied with string. "Open it."

Walter picked it up and turned it over. It was rectangular in shape and about an inch thick. "I wonder what it could be." He smiled, then untied the cord and handed it to his wife. It could be reused for something else. The same with the paper. It hadn't been taped but neatly folded. He took his time unwrapping the package to reveal what he hadn't purchased. Their first guest-book.

"Thank you, my dear. You think of everything. You're a lifesaver." Walter stood and kissed Mary on the cheek. "Had you given any thought as to where our guests would take breakfast?"

"I had thought in the formal dining room beside the living room. But perhaps they'd feel more comfortable in a family situation. We could always ask them where they'd prefer to break their fast. We'd have to ask them on check-in, though. That way, if it's the dining room, I can have the table laid ahead of time."

So far, nothing was mentioned about last night's episode. Grace appeared to be her usual happy self and not affected by the experience. He wouldn't mention it to Mary until they were alone.

"When you've finished your breakfast, Grace, go brush your teeth, then you can play in your room," Mary said.

"Yes, Mother. Does Clara have to brush her teeth, too?"

Walter rolled his eyes, and Mary had to look away before she laughed. "Yes. We can't have either one of you getting cavities. Dentist visits are very expensive."

Grace clambered down from her seat, snatched her doll from the high chair and dashed out of the room.

"How was she after you stayed with her?" Walter asked.

Mary sat at the table beside him. "She was asleep again in moments." She paused and topped up her coffee cup. "The room was cold during the night. I thought perhaps it was coming from an open window. I got up and checked, but the windows were closed. I had closed them before we retired for the night. It had rained earlier, and I didn't want it coming in. I'm not sure what caused it."

"I do hope it was just a bad dream," Walter said. "Yesterday was a stressful day. Even for Grace. Old houses. The cold could have come from about anywhere. Chimney flue, drafty windows."

"I hope she copes with having strangers in the house. We have our first guests arriving sometime this afternoon." Mary sipped her drink.

"Where are you putting them?"

"I originally thought about the room next to Grace's, but after last night, I think I'll move them to the last bedroom on the same side of the hall. The one with the small private bathroom."

"Good choice." Walter finished his meal and drained the coffee from his mug. "I'm going to have a putter in the grounds. Make sure everything is looking ship shape." He stood and kissed his wife.

After he left the kitchen, Mary sighed. The chill she felt in Grace's bedroom wasn't a cold night. There was more to it. If something happened again tonight, they would have to think about moving their daughter to a different room. Or even into their room, although that was a habit she didn't want to start. Maybe she could move her into the one next door. The one she thought of using for their guests. Until something happened, there was no point worrying about it.

Mary cleared the table and stacked the dishes on the counter. Before washing them, she wanted to ensure everything in the snug and guest bedroom was in order.

As Mary passed Grace's bedroom, she listened at the door. Her daughter was speaking to her doll. She couldn't make out the words, but nothing going on in the room was worrying. She continued down the corridor. Everything was fine in the room she selected for the visitors. Plenty of towels in the bathroom. Soap. Toilet paper, and extra rolls, too. The bedroom had been dusted and polished, and crisp white dresser skirts adorned with embroidery covered the surface of the dressing table and chest of drawers. She'd thought of everything. Mary opened the window to let fresh air into the space so it wouldn't be stale and stuffy.

On her way downstairs to check that everything in the snug was in order, a woman's weeping came from within Grace's room. She passed it off as Grace, pretending that Clara was crying about something. Ghosts didn't exist. The house was old and had lain empty for years. The sounds could be anything.

Inside the snug, Mary picked up the glasses she and Walter had used the previous evening. Once she washed and polished them, she'd return them to the tray. The room was cozy. Her guests would appreciate that. A cabinet radio stood inside the door. This room held a combination of the Kembleford's furnishings and their own. The wireless was theirs; the mahogany desk and leather chairs by the window came with the house. Same with the small table. Even the painting on the wall was original to the house. Most of the furniture she and Walter brought was in the large room off the kitchen, which they would use most of the time. They didn't have nearly enough furniture to fill this house. Most surprisingly, the contents weren't sold off after the bank foreclosed. She assumed the furnishings would have been sold at auction to recoup some of the lost money.

When she turned to leave, the aroma of cigar smoke filled the air. There was no bluish haze like you would expect in a smokey room, but the smell lingered. It was strong enough as if the smoker stood next to her. She quickened her pace and left the room.

By the time she reached the kitchen, her heart raced. Imagination. It had to be. What else? Mary braced herself against the counter. She needed to get a grip. Walter didn't need her acting like a lunatic. She filled the large cast iron sink with hot, soapy water and washed the dishes. Should she mention her strange encounters to her husband? Not today. Not when it was their first day as hoteliers.

Mary returned the glasses to the snug and checked the other rooms on the main floor which were spotless. After yesterday's reception, she wanted to ensure she hadn't missed cleaning up anything. That wouldn't make a good first impression.

Gravel crunched on the driveway. Their guests were early. What should she do? Walter went outside after breakfast so he'd be available to help with luggage. She smoothed the front of her house dress and walked to the vestibule door. The outer door was open. Likely left that way by her husband. It was summer, so it wasn't too cold to open doors and windows.

Mary paused by the mirror in the main hall and checked her hair. She appeared presentable. Did she greet them at the door? Stand behind the registration desk Walter built for them? It was all new to her, and he was outdoors puttering in the yard or one of the many flowerbeds. She opted to be ready to check them in and show them to the room she'd chosen.

The couple were around her age, judging by their appearance. The wife, wearing a pillbox hat, white cardigan over a blue print dress, and gloves, looked up at the ceilings and peered into the formal dining room before standing beside her husband. His dark brown hair was greying at the temples, and his green eyes sparkled when he smiled. She was a dark ash blonde with hazel eyes and remained silent. After brief eye contact with Mary, the woman turned away. It was as if she were nervous.

"We're on our way to the wife's mother's. When I looked on the map, Pike Falls seemed to be about the halfway point, so here we are," he said. "Bill Rankin, and this is my wife, Doris."

"Very nice to meet you both. I'm Mary Birkhoefer,

and you've probably met my husband already. His name is Walter. If you haven't, you'll meet him soon enough. If I could just get you to fill out your details in the register, including the year, make and model of your car, and the licence plate number."

While Bill completed the registration for their room, Mary retrieved their key from behind the desk.

"If you're ready, I'll show you to your room. I've put you in room five at the back of the house so you won't be bothered. It also has a private bathroom."

Mary led the way upstairs and to the couple's accommodations. "You'll want an early breakfast tomorrow since you're travelling again?"

"If it's not too much bother."

"None at all. Would seven o'clock suit you?"

"That would be fine, thanks."

"And you can eat in the formal dining room. I believe you saw it already, Mrs. Rankin. Or, you can eat with us in our kitchen. As long as you let me know before morning."

Mary concluded the tour of their room and showed the woman where extra blankets and pillows were located, along with additional personal supplies.

Doris followed Mary to the door and closed it behind her. The room was more than adequate. Still, there was something about the entire place that bothered her. She couldn't put her finger on it, but she was relieved they would only spend one night here. By this time tomorrow, they would be at her mother's house.

"What's wrong, honey?" Bill asked.

"I don't like this place. It's not the landlady. I like her fine, it's the building. There's something strange about it. Spooky."

"It's probably close to a hundred years old. Maybe that's why you think it's strange."

He had that look in his eye. That same look he got any time she mentioned 'spooky.' "Don't." Doris walked away from him and stared out the window.

The lawn was a lush emerald green and had recently been cut. The flower beds that bordered the stone wall surrounding the property were a full blaze of reds, yellows, and oranges. A man, who on their arrival, she thought was the gardener, looked up and waved. Doris shrank back, not wanting to be seen, and drew the curtains.

Doris had experienced strange things before. Bill laughed at her on those occasions, saying it was all in her head. Maybe he didn't believe in ghosts and haunted houses, but she did. Kembleford Manor was haunted, no matter what her husband said.

"Shall we go downstairs? We don't need to stay cooped up in our room. Take a walk around the grounds. Maybe go into the town?"

Doris nodded. Getting away from this place was the best idea Bill had. She picked up her handbag and started for the door. The sooner she was out of this house, the happier she would be.

Walter was cleaning the soles of his shoes on the boot scraper mounted on the front step when the couple opened the door. "Off for a wander?" he asked.

"Yes. We haven't met. Bill and Doris Rankin." Bill extended his hand to Walter.

"Walter Birkhoefer. Pleased to meet you both. I hope you enjoy your stay. Is your room adequate? My wife said she was putting you in room five with the private bathroom."

"Yes, it's fine," Doris replied.

"When you return from your wanderings, join me in the snug. It's that room right there. When you go in, turn to your right at the hall and it's the first door. It will be open. It's a cozy place. Great for a drink and a natter."

"We'd love to, wouldn't we, Doris?"

"I-I, yes."

"Off you go then. Enjoy."

Feet cleaned sufficiently to meet Mary's inspection, Walter headed into the house. The Rankins seemed like a lovely couple from his first impression. The missus seemed a bit nervous, though. However, things could change once he'd spent more time with them. The *Pike Falls Courier* wasn't published until the next day and he was anxious to read the coverage of the grand opening the reporter had written. Nervous, too. What if it wasn't positive? What if people wouldn't stay here because of his German heritage?

Bill gave his arm to Doris, and they set out. They hadn't reached the end of the long driveway when he stopped walking and faced her. "What's gotten into you, Doris? You were keen to stay at the Kembleford Manor Hotel when I first suggested it. Now, you're against it. Well? Tell me."

"For one thing, it's the house."

"I think it's a lovely place."

"You would. There's something that I can't quite put my finger on, but something bad happened there. I can feel it."

"Don't start that nonsense again."

"It's not nonsense, Bill. It's not evil but a profound sadness."

Bill shook his head. When his wife got these notions in her head, there was no swaying her. The house is old. People have lived it for at least a century. People died in it, too, no doubt. "What else bothers you about the place?"

"Their name. Birkhoefer. That's a German name."

"So?"

"The war? Hitler? Should we even be thinking of staying there?"

"I can't believe you just said that. It's disgusting. You can't paint the Birkhoefers with the same brush. They seem like a nice couple."

"You don't know on what side their loyalties lie. They could be supporters, sympathizers."

Again, Bill shook his head, shocked by the words coming out of his wife's mouth. He'd never seen this side of her. Not even when the war was taking place. "It's only one night. Let's just make the best of it, and whatever you do, don't cause a scene and mention any of what you just told me to them." He shoved his hands in his trouser pockets and hung his head. Kicked at a few stones as he continued towards the heart of the village.

Chapter Eighteen

JULY 1, 1947

After their walk through Pike Falls, Doris appeared more relaxed. That was until they reached the driveway of the Kembleford Manor Hotel. They'd held hands for most of their walk, but her hand tensed in his on their return. "What's wrong, dear?" Bill asked.

"Nothing. You think it's all my imagination except my feelings towards Walter since he's German."

"You aren't going to let that go are you. He's a friendly man and seriously wants to make a go of his hotel. You like his wife. Let's just make the best of things, and we'll be on our way to your mother's after breakfast."

The outside door was still open, but the inner one remained closed. Once across the vestibule, Bill opened the second door and stood aside so Doris could enter ahead of him. "Where did Walter say the snug was located? Oh, right. I remember. First door on the right when we get to the hallway."

He found the room with no problem and ushered his wife inside. It was cozy, as he'd been told earlier. A pair of leather chairs sat by the window next to a table with crystal glassware and a matching decanter set on top. Another seating area lay kitty-corner to this one and between an enormous mahogany desk filled the space. A cabinet stood along the wall under a giant portrait. Bill walked towards it for a closer look. Sometimes, on old paintings, a brass plaque was affixed to the frame with details of the person portrayed. In this case, there was nothing.

"Ah, I thought I heard voices. Will you join me for a drink? I have some cognac, brandy, and some fine single malts from Scotland."

"I wouldn't say no to a whisky, Walter."

"Fine then. And you? Doris, isn't it?"

"Yes, and brandy, please."

"Please sit. My wife will join us shortly."

Bill seated his wife in one of the chairs by the window and sat in the other.

Doris watched Walter pour the drinks. She wanted to ensure he didn't slip anything into either one and poison them. Say, like cyanide. From what she'd read and heard on the radio news, it was a favourite of the Germans.

Satisfied that Walter hadn't poisoned her brandy, Doris accepted the glass. She passed it under her nose as an extra precaution. At that moment, Mary joined them. "Did you have a lovely walk through the town?" she asked.

"Yes. It was most enjoyable," said Doris.

"Pike Falls is very picturesque. We saw the river, but is there actually a waterfall? We didn't see that," replied Bill.

"Ah, the Pike River, yes. Now, we've not seen the falls but apparently, they are upriver, well north of the town. We've been so busy fixing this place up, we haven't had much of a chance to sightsee. There is a boathouse at the back of the property, but we've not even looked inside it," said Walter.

"I must say, you've done a wonderful job on the house," said Doris.

"Most of the work was cleaning," Mary replied. "To say it had lain abandoned since 1914, it was in remarkable condition."

"Pardon me, but your accent. It's not German like your husband's."

"No, Mrs. Rankin, it isn't. I'm of Irish descent. It makes for some interesting discussions when the family gets together. You see, my father had no use for Germans. Couldn't stand them. Then I came home with one as my fiancé. Well, he got to know Walter and eventually gave his blessing for our marriage. The rest of the villagers weren't as understanding. I think they got a petition together to drive Walter out of the village. He had been looking for an opportunity to go into business for himself, and Quabbinville wasn't the place to do that."

"Is this Quabbinville close?" asked Doris. The heat from her flush burned her cheeks, embarrassed by Mary's candour.

"No, thankfully," said Walter. "The only way I'd be able to run a successful business was to be far from those narrow-minded residents. I saw a small notice in the newspaper about this place coming up for auction. Mary and I discussed it, and here we are. The rest, as they say, is history."

"It's a remarkable story. Do you know much about the property's history?" Bill asked.

Doris turned to her husband.

"I only know the gossip. The home was purchased by Albert Kembleford, the founder of the Kembleford Lumber Mill. He shot himself, they say, right in this room."

A chill raced up Doris's spine. "I-in h-here?"

"Yes. Now that's only gossip, you understand," said Walter.

"It was a reporter from the local newspaper who told us that. We had no idea until yesterday. He asked us if we believed in the Kembleford Curse," Mary said. "Then he told us about the daughter who killed herself because her baby died."

"I can see why the rumour of a curse started," Doris said as she started to stand. "I've had enough for now. I think I'd like to lie down." She tipped her glass back and drained the remainder of the brandy.

The distinct aroma of cigar smoke filled the room. The others didn't seem to notice it, or if they did, it was a regular occurrence, and they'd grown used to it. Strangely, Bill seemed oblivious to it as well. Was she the only one who could smell it? She made her excuses and slipped out of the room.

Bill was content to let Doris head off to their room alone. He enjoyed speaking with their hosts. "If you don't mind me asking, Walter, how old were you when you came to Canada?" He swirled the whisky in his glass before he sipped. Allowing that bit of air to make its way into the liquid changed the flavour. Bill was no whisky snob, and he couldn't place where he'd heard or seen people do it.

"Let me think. I was ... no, I was about ten. My brother, Friedrich, was younger than me. We thought it was a great adventure."

"I imagine you would."

"Mother was totally against us leaving Germany. I shouldn't say that. She was open to leaving, just not sailing. *RMS Titanic* had struck an iceberg and sank. *RMS Lusitania* was torpedoed by the Germans and sank in May of 1915, almost a year to the day before we sailed. Mother always said, 'I'll follow you anywhere, Valter, but not across the ocean.'"

"Well, it would seem she did just that, or did you and your brother come with only your father?"

"No, Mother relented, and our family travelled together. Can I top up your whisky?"

Mary excused herself and left the room.

"Thank you," Bill said as he held out his glass. "I found this period in history fascinating, not just because of the war. I mean, there were so many lives affected by it. Loved ones off fighting. Some never returned. And the relentless bombing. How could you not be interested?"

"Unlike during the Second World War that we've just come through, back then, we didn't have blackout curtains, air raid sirens or bomb shelters. Our village had a half dozen spotters who let us know of incoming planes. My father owned a bakery, and we lived in the apartment above it. Our property was never bombed, but nearby ones were, and neighbours we knew were killed. Mother wanted to escape all that, but it was impossible since she didn't want to cross the ocean." Walter sipped his drink.

"I never thought of that. I assumed those things been around and thrust back into service for this latest battle."

Bill stood and walked to where the huge portrait hung. "This any relation to you?"

"No. We inherited the painting, like most of the goods and chattels on the property. We think the man might be Albert Kembleford or maybe his father, but we don't know anyone who was around back at the time and knew him."

"Shame. It's a handsome piece of art."

"That it is."

"Well, Walter, I've kept you long enough with all this talk of war and ocean voyages. I need to find Doris."

"It's been a pleasure, Bill. I enjoy meeting people, and you haven't kept me from anything." Walter stood and shook his guest's hand.

Walter gathered the empty glasses and took them to the kitchen. Mary was busy and didn't hear him come in. At least, she never indicated that she knew he was in the room. He set the glassware on the counter and put his arms around his wife's waist. She shrieked.

"Walter, what do you mean sneaking up on me like that? You scared me half to death."

"I'm sorry, my love. A moment of madness. The roast beef smells delicious."

"Oh my, the roast! I got busy with other things and forgot about it. I hope it's not burned to a crisp." She pulled the oven door open using her apron. The pan was too hot for only it. "Potholders, please, Walter."

He removed them from the hook and handed them to his wife.

The flavourful steam filled the room. Walter leaned over the roast pan for a better sniff. Also in the juices with the chunk of beef were potatoes, onions, turnips, and carrots. "I can't wait to get tucked into this. You've outdone yourself this time, Mary dearest."

"Are the Rankins eating here tonight or elsewhere?" Mary asked.

"I'm not sure. We had a lovely conversation,

especially Bill and me, but it never occurred to ask them about eating with us tonight. I'll pop up to their room and ask."

"And if they want the formal dining room or out here with us," Mary called after him.

Walter took the back stairs to reach the room the Rankins were staying in. As he approached, the sounds of raised voices wafted towards him. The walls muffled the sound so he couldn't hear what was being said. He paused for a moment outside the room, then knocked. Three sharp raps.

"Who is it?" called Doris from the other side.

"Walter. Mary wanted to know if you'd be taking your evening meal here tonight. And if so, would you like to eat in the formal dining room or join our family? Mary has a pot roast simmering."

The idea of pot roast appealed to Doris. If only they wouldn't have to spend time with Walter. Her husband was practically salivating at the meal choice, so she knew his answer.

"We'd love to. And in the formal dining room, please," Doris said.

"I'll let Mary know. Come down when you're ready. Dinner should be about half an hour from now."

When the sound of retreating footsteps reached Doris's ears, she breathed a sigh of relief. Walter wasn't the only reason she didn't like this place, although he was top of the list. The cigar smoke smell and the profound sadness ranked right up there with them. And the gossip about the place. Two suicides. Albert Kembleford followed later by his daughter due to the death of her child, and no doubt her father as well.

Doris picked up her cardigan and slipped it over her shoulders. The sleeveless dress wasn't quite enough inside. She and Bill left their room and turned towards the main stairs. A soft voice sang when they reached the room at the end of the corridor. She paused and listened. The melody sounded vaguely familiar, but the tone of the voice was sorrowful. The door opened, and a small girl carrying a china doll stepped out. No way the singer was this child. She was too young to have a voice so developed.

"Are you the people who are staying with us?" she asked

"Yes, we are. My name is Doris, and my husband's name is Bill."

"My name is Grace, and this is Clara," she said, indicating her doll.

"It's a pleasure to meet you, Grace, and Clara, too," Doris said.

Grace bounded off down the stairs, leaving the Rankins in the hallway.

The melancholy voice resumed its song. A chill ran up Doris's spine, and she rushed to the head of the staircase.

When they reached the dining room, the table was laid with fine bone china bearing a floral pattern, sterling silver flatware, and crystal glasses. A crystal pitcher filled with water sat in the middle of the table. The tablecloth was so white it was almost blinding.

"This room is beautiful. I think we'll have breakfast here tomorrow before we check out," Doris said. What she didn't say was it can't come soon enough.

"It's quite the house. Walter and Mary have made it welcoming. I hope they're successful."

"I imagine they will be if the ghosts of the past don't ruin it for them."

"Are you back on that tangent again?"

"Yes. Just before the little girl came out of her room, I heard a woman singing softly from there. It wasn't the child. I've yet to see a radio anywhere but in the snug. It had to be a ghost."

Bill seated his wife and then sat across from her where the other place setting had been laid out. He picked up the pitcher and poured himself a glass of water. "Want some?" When Doris nodded, he filled hers, too.

Kitchen noises became louder, and Mary arrived

with a tureen of the same pattern as the place settings. "The roast is done a little more than I wanted. I'm sorry for that."

"I'm sure it will be fine."

Mary sat the huge vessel on the table and backed out, leaving them to their meal.

Doris lifted the tureen's lid and ladled herself a serving of the pot roast, which was more like stew. She handed the ladle to Bill, and he served himself.

"I forgot the homemade buns and butter," Mary said when she returned. "It wouldn't be a proper meal without them. And I have apple pie for dessert. You can have it with cheese or ice cream. Let me know when I come back to clear away the dishes."

Lowering her eyes, Doris began her supper. The food was delicious. Despite the pot roast being more stew-like, the meat melted in her mouth, and the carrots, turnips and potatoes were tender and flavourful. If Mary cooked like this every day, it was surprising the family wasn't overweight. Yet, they were all slim.

Bill sighed as he ate. Doris knew she wasn't the best cook but she was learning. With a meal like this to live up to when they finally returned home, she wasn't sure if she could create anything as spectacular. The kitchen in their apartment was tiny. Mary had to have a huge kitchen with large ovens — perhaps even a restaurant kitchen with all the latest gadgets.

Mary returned a short time later and cleared away their dishes. When she returned with their dessert, both chose ice cream to accompany their warm apple pie; she invited them to join her and Walter in the snug for tea and coffee afterward.

"I'm glad you decided to join us. We might be going a bit overboard with our hospitality, so please say so, but you're our first guests so we're not sure." Mary fidgeted with a napkin on her lap.

A silver teapot sat on the cabinet radio and a coffee urn beside it. Cream and sugar, cups and saucers, spoons and tongs, too. Doris poured herself a cup of tea and sat in one of the chairs, leaving the one between her and Walter for her husband.

"It's different," said Bill, "but then we've never stayed in a small hotel like this. Family run and oriented. Any of our other stays have been in larger hotels and motels where the service is impersonal."

"I think you'll take your cue from your guests. If they seem aloof and don't respond to your friendliness, then you'll have to tone it down. I agree with Bill. We've never stayed in a small hotel where we can mingle with the hosts. It's enjoyable," Doris said.

"We should have an early night, dear. It's another long drive again tomorrow."

"You're right, Bill." Doris took a final sip of her tea and placed her cup and saucer on the table.

He helped his wife out of her chair, and they said their goodnights.

After they left the room, Mary followed, closed the door, and leaned against it. "I'm not sure about this, Walter. Yesterday and today have been exhausting. It didn't help with Grace's nightmare last night. When I stayed with her, I slept lightly so I'd be there with her if she woke from another bad dream."

"It's early days. You'll get a routine worked out. When I'm not gardening, I can help you inside."

"Can I hold you to that, Walter?"

"Yes, dear. Why don't I help you take these things through to the kitchen and we'll wash them up and set the dining room up for morning. Then we'll go to bed."

Mary sighed. She hoped Walter's helpful streak lasted. His domesticity came in fits and starts and never stayed long. She switched off the light and closed the snug door behind her.

They hadn't reached the kitchen when a blood-curdling scream sounded from upstairs. Mary dropped the tray with the teapot and coffee urn. It crashed on the floor and the contents from the two vessels spewed into the air and splattered on the walls. Somehow, Walter had managed to get to the kitchen with the other dishes. No crash from there, but he raced back into the hall.

"What was that, Mary?"

"I believe it was Grace," she said, too stunned to move.

"Come, we'll see what's wrong."

Walter was halfway up the stairs before Mary was able to put one foot in front of the other. As she ascended the staircase, Bill and Doris and their luggage were coming down.

"We're not staying. How much do we owe you?" Doris asked. "This is just too much. Your hotel is haunted and I think your daughter is possessed by the devil."

"No charge. You didn't stay," Mary said, weariness filled her voice.

When she reached Grace's bedroom, the little girl was sitting cross-legged on the floor rocking back and forth. Her eyes were glassy and she had a darkening red mark on her left cheek.

"What happened, sweetheart? How did you get that mark on your face?"

"Th-that lady. Th-the one who tried to steal Cl-Clara. It was her."

"Where's Clara now?"

"I don't know. That lady took her. Said she wasn't Clara. She was Anna."

Mary crouched down and gathered her daughter into her arms. "Walter, look for Clara. I'll get Grace settled."

When she tried to tuck the little girl into bed, she was met with resistance. "No! No! No!" Grace screeched. "I don't want to stay in this room. That lady will come back."

"I'm sure it was only a dream, sweetie." Mary wasn't convinced herself. Dreams didn't hit you and leave marks.

"Do you want to sleep in the bedroom next door? I'll bring your pillow and blanket in so it will be like your bed."

"No," Grace yelled. "I don't want to live here. I hate this place. I hate that lady."

It was going to be a long night. Finally, Mary

bundled her up and took her to hers and Walter's bedroom. At least she met with less opposition now. Before long, Grace was sound asleep under the sheets and duvet.

Mary flopped in the armchair in the corner. Was there something to the Kembleford curse? Was this 'lady' Grace saw on more than one occasion the ghost of Ophelia Kembleford mourning the loss of her baby? The idea seemed too far-fetched, but what other explanation was there?

Walter returned to find his daughter asleep in his and Mary's bed and his wife sleeping in the armchair. He didn't want to wake either of them, but since he needed to discuss tonight's disturbance, he had no choice.

"Mary, wake up," he whispered in her ear.

She woke with a start.

"I'm sorry. I didn't mean to startle you. Can we talk? Not in here. I don't want to wake Grace."

Mary pulled herself up from the chair. "Where?"

"Kitchen. If Grace wakes up, we'll hear her."

He escorted Mary downstairs. The wreckage from earlier remained on the hall floor. She pulled away from him. "Leave it until morning. We'll clean it up then. You and me."

Mary nodded.

"What happened after I went looking for Clara?"

"Grace told me she hates her room, hates this house, and hates that lady. She has a bruise starting on her face. I don't know how she got it. She said that lady hit her."

Walter absorbed his wife's words. Something was definitely amiss here in Kembleford Manor. He still didn't believe in the curse the reporter mentioned to him. That was utter nonsense, or was it?

"She told me the lady said Clara was Anna."

Was it possible? Walter was a black and white kind of guy. There were no grey areas. One or the other and nothing in between. "Anna, I wonder if that was the stillborn child?" he mused. "Remember, the reporter mentioned it yesterday." Was it only yesterday? It seemed so much had happened since then, that it felt more like a month ago.

"Did you find Clara?"

Walter jumped. He had been lost in thought about the previous occupants of the house and his wife's voice startled him.

"No. I've looked in all the rooms, under the furniture. She's not in this house."

"We must find her. Grace will be devastated if she's gone. Did you look in the tower?"

"No. That was the one place I didn't look." Walter stood and he and his wife climbed the stairs to their room. He opened the door that led into an anteroom between the two principle bedrooms on the front of the house. He turned the light switch but nothing happened. "I need a lantern."

Mary lit the oil lamp they kept on their highboy and handed it to him.

Walter made his way to the spiral staircase and slowly climbed until he reached the tower room. He'd never been up here. It was unfinished. The beams and rafters exposed and covered in cobwebs. He'd have to close it off so that Grace didn't get up here. If she did, she could end up having another asthma attack and wind up in the hospital. Beneath the grimy window, lay a cradle. He approached cautiously. There, tucked in under the blankets was Clara. Walter picked up the china doll and started towards the staircase. He turned back towards the cradle. First, he'd get Grace's doll returned to her then he'd retrieve the cradle, clean it up and maybe if it was in a portion of the house that was used, if Clara went missing again, she'd be easier to find.

Chapter Nineteen

JULY 2, 1947

It was well past midnight by the time Walter returned with Clara. After a quick inspection, Mary tucked the doll under the blankets with Grace. He disappeared into the anteroom again and returned with a cradle.

"Come, we'll take this and go downstairs," he whispered.

Mary extinguished the oil lamp and followed him down to the kitchen. It would be another sleepless night, by the looks of things. By the time she arrived, he had the cradle on the counter inspecting it. The mattress pad and bedding were in a heap on the floor.

"I'm going to close off access to the tower from both bedrooms. I'll clean this up, and we'll put it in Grace's room, and Clara can have a new bed. One which, if she disappears again, we'll find her in but in a used part of the house. The other things will need to be washed, too. They're dusty from being up there."

"It's all so bizarre, Walter. I don't know what to make of it. Is our house truly haunted? I can't believe it."

"I don't believe so." He returned to cleaning the dust and cobwebs from the cradle.

"I'm going to see Mrs. Pritchard later. I'll ask her if she can help us out for a while. We have more guests coming over the next few days, and the Rankin's room will have to be made up again; we've not slept, and I've got that mess in the hall."

"That's fine, dear. Do you want anything? Tea? Coffee?"

She was wide awake now and couldn't sleep for quite some time. "Coffee would be lovely." She sank onto a chair at the table and watched her husband prepare a pot of coffee in their percolator. Walter was a good man. He was good with his hands and able to build almost anything. He was an excellent father to Grace. The man couldn't boil water, as the expression went, but he made a decent pot of coffee.

"How do you propose to block off the access?" Mary asked.

"I'll fill in the doorway on our side of the anteroom. Do it from inside there. We'll keep the door locked and move a piece of furniture across it."

"And on the other side?"

"I can't do anything on that side until ours is done. I'll need a way to get back out. That will require more pondering."

Mary sipped the brew her husband sat in front of her. If there was a way to block access to keep everyone, but especially Grace, out of there, he'd find it.

Mary dozed at the table, her chin propped on her hand.

"A priest hole," Walter shouted.

She snapped out of her light sleep. "What?"

"A priest hole. But instead of underground, I'll build it into the back of the wardrobe in the other front bedroom. Close the wall around it to look solid like the rest of the room, but a secret passage in the back of the cupboard will remain solid unless a tiny switch is released, and then it will open."

"And how will it stay open after you get in there?"

"Details, details. Let me get to work on it. Paper, paper. I need paper. A pencil and a straight edge, too."

Mary gathered the requested items and set them out on the table. She stood behind him and watched over his shoulder. If someone did that to her, it would drive her crazy, but her husband was so engrossed in his work that she doubted he even knew she was there. Walter sat and sketched furiously with notes on his invention along the margins.

"Mother, Daddy, you found Clara! I love you," Grace yelled from the doorway.

The grandfather clock in the hall chimed six o'clock. Today would be a long day.

"Where did you find her?"

"Your father found her sleeping in this cradle. He's going to clean it up, and I'll launder the bedding, and then Clara will have a new bed. Maybe we can put it in the living room? Would you like that?"

"Yes, please, Mother," Grace said as she hugged her mother.

"Hop up to the table, and I'll get your breakfast. I'm going over to Mrs. Pritchard's today. Would you like to come with me?"

"Yes, please."

Mrs. Pritchard would love to see Grace, and her ulterior motive of getting her daughter out of the house would allow Walter to work on his projects in peace and perhaps even secrecy. Grace didn't need to know what her father was doing, and if she had known, she'd have wanted to explore the tower room, which was too dangerous.

Mary wouldn't leave until eight o'clock. That way, she wouldn't interrupt the woman's breakfast rush at her boarding house, and it would give her time to clean up the mess in the hall. Once she had Grace settled with a bowl of cereal, she went out into the corridor and retrieved the urn and the teapot. Neither was damaged from being dropped. That was a relief. It was an expense they couldn't afford at the moment since she didn't charge the Rankins for their non-stay. Unless he could find materials, Walter would need to buy the things he needed to block access to the tower.

The wall didn't look too splattered. There couldn't have been much left in either pot when Mary dropped the tray. Maybe the disaster wasn't as bad as she thought.

Eight o'clock came, and Mary and Grace set out for Mrs. Pritchard's boarding house. Grace pushed a doll carriage with Clara ensconced under a crocheted blanket and flannel sheet.

Despite the early hour, it was warm. The sun, still not high in the sky, beat down on them. Mary took a handkerchief from her handbag and blotted it against her forehead. Birdsong filled the air, although she didn't see any birds. With the trees and hedges leafed out, they could be hidden in them and probably remain comfortable, not sweating like she was.

The walk from Kembleford Manor to the boarding house took about fifteen minutes. Mary went around to the back door, knowing that Mrs. Pritchard would be in her kitchen. She knocked on the screen door and called, "Hello."

"Come in," a voice replied from somewhere inside.

Mary ensured the doll carriage stayed outside but allowed Grace to bring Clara into the warm kitchen. A stack of plates next to the sink indicated that her friend was clearing up the breakfast rush.

"Hi, Grandma Pritchard," Grace said when the woman entered the kitchen with an armload of linens.

"Hello, Grace. How are you today?"

"I'm fine now that Clara is found."

"Found? I didn't know she was lost."

"I'll tell you about it later," Mary said. "It looks like we caught you at a bad time."

"I always have time for a visit with my two favourite people. Would you like a coffee, Mary?"

"I'd love one."

"And how about you, Grace, a nice glass of milk and one of my soft molasses cookies?"

"Yes, please."

There was a never-ending supply of coffee, conversation, and treats for children here. Mary had never managed that balance. Either the coffee turned out bitter, or the baking ran out. She'd have to be better coordinated now that she had guests coming and going. Today's people thought they would arrive after four o'clock when they telephoned to request a room. Walter must have advertised in every newspaper in the province. Well, at least the major ones. Between taking out ads and putting in a telephone, they spent a significant amount of their savings. At least they didn't have a party line like Mrs. Pritchard.

By now, Grace had finished her milk and cookie, so Mary sent her out into the backyard to play. This conversation she didn't want to have in front of her daughter.

Mary sighed with relief when the screen door shut behind Grace. "I need to ask a huge favour of you."

"What might that be?"

"Walter and I haven't slept much these past few nights. Grace's sleep has been disturbed ...," she trailed off while formulating the next portion of her sentence, "by terrifying nightmares."

"Oh dear."

"I'm not sure what's causing them. Grace didn't have them when we stayed here with you."

"Grace is more than welcome to stay here with me. There's always room for her. You and Walter, too, if you need to get away from the hotel."

"That's very kind of you." Mary gripped her coffee mug with both hands. The heat from the hot liquid was soothing. "No, but would you be available a few hours a day for the next while? So I can get into some sort of routine with people coming and going."

"Of course, dear." Mrs. Pritchard patted Mary's shoulder.

"You seem to have everything so under control here. I wish I was that coordinated."

"I have my days when everything I touch goes to hell in a handbasket."

Mary suppressed a laugh. It didn't seem possible that this woman had bad days. What did surprise her was the turn of phrase she used. She'd never heard the woman swear or even say damn before. She learned something new about her friend.

"Grace mentioned Clara being found. Was she lost?"

"Yes." Mary sighed. "That's part of the reason for Grace's disturbed sleep. She insists a lady came into her room twice and tried to take Clara away from her, saying she didn't belong to Grace that she was hers. The last time it happened, Grace had a huge red mark on her cheek. That blotch was gone this morning. Anyway, this time, the lady Grace saw said the baby's name was Anna and not Clara, and she took her."

"Oh my. But you found Clara. Where?"

"Walter found her up in the tower in an old cradle."

"There's something you should know. My mother was the Nursery Maid for the Kemblefords after their daughter Ophelia was born. She stayed until well after Lavinia's birth. Then, she started the boarding house here to bring in money. My father had died shortly before she started working for the Kemblefords. Later on, when Ophelia became pregnant, they hired her back. I was old enough to look after this place. Are you okay, dear? You're looking a bit peaky."

"I'm fine. Please go on. I want to hear the rest of it." Mary retrieved her handkerchief from her bag. She felt she might need it before Mrs. Pritchard finished her story.

"Now, where was I? Oh, yes. The day Albert Kembleford killed himself, the shock sent Ophelia into premature labour, and the baby was stillborn."

"And that baby was named Anna."

"Yes."

"Do you think this is the cause of Grace's nightmares? I never mentioned anything to Walter, but I have smelled cigar smoke quite strong in the room we use as the snug and in the corridors. Did Mr. Kembleford smoke them?"

"Yes. My mother was always after him to not smoke them around the small children."

"If you knew about all this, why didn't you say something before?" Mary leapt to her feet.

"What good would it have done? You wouldn't have believed me. You would have thought I was a dotty old lady. I never believed in what the newspapers called the Kembleford Curse. And neither should you."

Mary sank back onto the chair. She would have

to tell Walter about this. Their home couldn't be haunted by two members of the Kembleford family, could it? The more she thought about it, the less angry she was with Mrs. Pritchard. The woman only told her about the tragedies the previous occupants suffered. Nothing at all related to ghostly occurrences. But, she did avoid answering the question related to Grace's nightmares. It could all be a coincidence, but at least she had some insight into the previous owners.

"Do you still want my help a few hours a day?" Mrs. Pritchard asked.

"Please. I best be on my way. I've kept you long enough."

"Do take care, dear, and I'll pop over this afternoon after the lunchtime rush for a few hours."

"Thank you. You're a godsend." Mary hugged the woman, went outside to collect Grace and return home.

Chapter Twenty

Mary and Grace started for home. On their way, they met Dougie Smith on his bicycle, which had a huge basket on the front where he carried his newspapers on his Monday to Friday paper route.

"Hi, Mrs. Birkhoefer. Hi, Grace," he said as he pedalled past them. "I've already been to your house with your paper."

"Is there a write-up about our hotel opening in it?" Mary turned and called after him.

"You're on the front page, Mrs. Birkhoefer."

Mary's mouth tugged into a smile. Dougie was a lovely young boy. He wasn't yet a teenager but had to be at least eleven. They didn't hire anyone younger for a paper route. She picked up her pace, eager to get home and look at the newspaper and read the article.

Walter met them, waving the newspaper in the air. "Front page, Mary. We're on the front page," he exclaimed.

Mary, swept up in his excitement, hugged him tight. "I know. We met the paperboy and he told us. You deserve it, dearest. This has been your dream for so long, and now you're on the front page. Now, let me see it."

"Here it is. Isn't it wonderful?"

PIKE FALLS COURIER

Vol. 47127   Wednesday, July 2, 1947   One nickel

NEW LIFE BREATHED INTO HISTORIC MANSION

James Clancy, Staff Reporter

June 30, 1947, marked the beginning of a new era for Kembleford Manor. The former home of ruined lumber baron Albert Kembleford has received a new lease on life being reincarnated as the Kembleford Manor Hotel.

A ribbon-cutting ceremony marked the occasion with many Pike Falls dignitaries and local residents in attendance. This was followed by a tour of the small hotel and refreshments served in the formal dining room.

Mrs. Birkhoefer looked particularly resplendent in a modest, navy blue, short-sleeved shirtwaist dress with a tie belt, wrist-length white gloves, and brown mid-heel oxfords. Atop her head, she wore a simple white pillbox hat.

Despite the day's heat, Mr. Birkhoefer greeted people wearing a charcoal pinstripe double-breasted suit with cuffed trousers. The look was set off by a white shirt, black silk tie, and matching charcoal homburg hat. His black wing-tipped shoes gleamed in the sunlight.

Even their seven-year-old daughter joined them, looking every bit the proper young lady with her hair in braids with bows that matched her puffed, short-sleeved green party dress, white ankle socks and brown t-strap shoes.

The family from eastern Ontario had been looking for such an opportunity and were thrilled to discover this lovely manor house for sale.

Everything original to the house remains, although additional facilities have been added. Some rooms share bathrooms, while the larger suites have private ones.

A selection of finger sandwiches, canapés, and vol-au-vents made by Mrs. Birkhoefer were available along with champagne, fruit juices and tea or coffee.

When asked about the Kembleford Curse, Mr. Birkhoefer shook his head and laughed, saying he didn't believe in such things.

"I haven't read the entire article yet, Walter."

Mary scanned the piece. "Well, it's certainly favourable, although I didn't expect quite so much description of our appearance. He could have left out the nonsense about the Kembleford Curse, though."

Was the curse nonsense? It was debatable with the strange occurrences since they moved into the manor house. She wouldn't bother Walter with her conversation with Mrs. Pritchard right now. It would wait. She didn't want to ruin his excitement at their success in the news. Besides, she had work to do if she was going to have the room ready for the next guests scheduled to arrive later that afternoon.

"Mary, I've just had a wonderful idea. I'm going to get extra copies of The *Pike Falls Courier* and leave them at the reception desk. I'll contact the paper and have them deliver extras going forward."

"Can we afford the added expense? I doubt we'll be in the news every week."

"All right then. Just this once. Besides, we'll want to send some to the family."

She couldn't deny the satisfaction she'd feel once her father read the story. He might even share it with the narrow-minded people who forced them to leave. Wouldn't that make them sit up and take notice? "Mrs. Pritchard has agreed to help me out a few hours a day until we work out a routine."

"Wonderful, my dear. Hopefully, Grace will start sleeping better."

Mary's mind went back to her visit with the older woman. She needed to tell Walter about it before Mrs. Pritchard arrived this afternoon. She'd talk to him when he returned with extra copies of the paper.

Walter couldn't keep a straight face. Every time he tried, his lips curled back into a smile. He had the right to be happy. They succeeded at converting a former manor house into a hotel. They had guests already, and more arriving today and tomorrow. Now, if Grace slept through the night without incident, it would be miraculous. If they ended up moving her out of her current bedroom, maybe that would help. The small bedroom above the one they used as a snug seemed to be the catalyst behind his daughter's night terrors.

"Great article, Walter," the local haberdasher called as he passed the man's shop.

"Thank you," he replied.

This repeated itself all the way to the Pike Falls Courier office at the far end of Main Street. Inside the door, a rack held extra copies for non-subscribers to buy. Or, in this case, for subscribers to purchase extras. He picked up ten more. Better to have too many than not enough. He'd send one to his parents. Perhaps one to his grandparents back in Germany. One to his brother who eventually went to work on the railway and lived in Toronto. Mary would want to send one to her parents and possibly her grandparents. That didn't add up to ten copies, but there would be extras at the reception desk at their hotel.

Walter proudly carried the stack of papers he purchased home. He showed off the front page of the top newspaper to people he met on the street. His chest was so puffed out from the success of their opening that his buttons strained.

When he returned to the hotel, Mrs. Pritchard had already arrived. She was in the main hallway. The carpet runner was rolled up, and she was on her hands and knees scrubbing the hardwood.

"Mr. Birkhoefer, my floor! You're leaving footprints all over it," she scolded him.

"I'm sorry, Mrs. Pritchard. I'll go around and come in through the door back of the kitchen." He walked around the house and inspected the flowerbeds as he went. Periodically, he stopped and dead-headed a spent bloom. It was still early enough that the floor would be dried when their next guests arrived. He couldn't imagine entering a hotel and getting that greeting if he were a paying guest.

When he entered the kitchen, he called out for his wife, but there was no response. He left the papers on the table and walked down the secondary hall to the back stairs. He found Mary in room five, changing the bedding. A pile of towels, sheets and pillowcases were on the floor.

"Would you be a dear and take that laundry down to the kitchen for me, please?" she asked.

"Certainly, my dear. Do you need me to do anything for you in here?"

"No, thank you. I'm almost finished. I'd like to get that washed and out on the line while it's still nice. It's warm, and there's a breeze, so it will be a good drying day."

"I'll set the machine up by the sink then so it will be ready for you."

"Thanks. That will be a help."

Walter left his wife to finish up and returned to the kitchen with the armload of washing.

Mary filled the wringer washer with hot water from the kitchen faucet. As it filled, she added detergent and a bit of bleach. Once ready, she arranged the bedding and towels and started the machine. The view from her window over the sink calmed her. The fully leafed-out mature birch trees, with their white bark, contrasted with the vibrant hues in the flower gardens beyond. Walter had done a beautiful job getting them into shape. When they first arrived, the beds were overgrown and in a terrible state.

She needed to talk to Walter about the conversation she'd had earlier with Mrs. Pritchard, but he was off doing whatever he did when there were domestic chores. A stack of newspapers sat on the table. Mary let the machine work on its own and inspected them. There were more than enough to send home to family. Walter got carried away as usual. She skimmed over the article again and smiled. He had every right to be pleased.

"That's me away," Mrs. Pritchard said.

"You startled me."

"I'm sorry. I'm off now. The front hall is dry, and the runner laid out and swept. I had to wash it a second time because your husband walked on it and left footprints. I'll be back tomorrow at about the same time."

"Would you like a cup of coffee or tea before you leave?"

"No. Much as I would love one, I best get back to the boarding house and start preparing the supper. The men will be hungry and want to eat when they get home from work."

"See you tomorrow, then," Mary said to the older woman's back as she left the room and returned to the job at hand. The laundry had washed long enough, so she drained the water from the machine and refilled it to rinse. Once she decided that was sufficient, she passed it through the wringer and into the waiting clothes basket.

As Mary stepped out the kitchen door on her way to the clothesline, the figure of a dark-haired woman in a long white nightgown dashed across the lawn towards the boathouse. She turned and looked over her shoulder at the house. The woman was transparent. Mary could see the trees and flowerbeds through the woman's clothing and exposed face and hands. Startled by the sight, she dropped the laundry basket, and the clean towels and bedding tumbled onto the grass.

Mary continued to stare after the woman until she vanished. It wasn't one minute she was there and the next she wasn't. It was gradual, as if she merely faded away.

"Mother," Grace called her from the kitchen door, snapping Mary out of her reverie.

"Can I have a snack, please? I'm hungry."

"Let me get this lot on the line, and I'll get you something." Mary looked at the dropped load of washing. It landed on the grass. It shouldn't be dirty. She shook each piece to dislodge any bits of grass or other debris before hanging it on the line, then raised the pole in the middle to raise the clothesline higher.

Mary fixed Grace a snack of cheese and crackers and poured her a glass of cold milk. "You sit there at the table. I'm going to find your father."

"Yes, Mother."

Mary left Grace and started out into the hall. There was no mention of Clara. Whenever Grace wanted something, she always asked if Clara could have the same. She didn't notice the china doll in her daughter's arms or in the highchair Walter had made for it. Perhaps her daughter had grown less dependent on the doll? Or Clara was sleeping in the cradle up in Grace's room? That was the most logical explanation.

Walter was in the snug. "A bit early in the day, isn't it?" she asked.

"I'm merely reading the paper, my dear." He picked it up and gave it a shake.

"I had an interesting conversation with Mrs. Pritchard when Grace and I went to the boarding house this morning. Did you know her mother was the Nursery Maid for the Kemblefords?"

"No. I had no idea."

"Well, she was, and when Ophelia Kembleford gave birth prematurely to a stillborn daughter, she named her Anna."

"I remember the reporter mentioning something about that. It was the same day her father killed himself in this very room."

"Grace mentioned the name Anna after one of her encounters with, as she calls her, 'that lady.' What's going on here, Walter? Is our house haunted? Is the Kembleford Curse real?"

"I don't believe any of that. It's true Grace hasn't been herself. If we move her to a different bedroom, will it help? Her room is directly above here."

"I've heard sounds. Crying. Mournful singing. Smelled cigar smoke. And just now, when I went to hang out the laundry, I saw a woman in a long white nightgown. Dark-haired and running towards the boathouse. It was almost like she faded away when she realized I was watching her."

"I think you're overtired and worried. That's all. And this talk of the Kembleford Curse and Mrs. Pritchard's mother working for the family isn't helping."

Gravel crunched in the driveway. A taxi pulled up outside the window. "I do believe our guests are here."

"They're a bit early, aren't they?" Mary asked.

"No. It's just after four o'clock, and you told me that was the time they expected to arrive. Come along, dear. Can't keep them waiting."

The couple extracting themselves from the cab were older. Perhaps mid to late sixties like Mrs. Pritchard. The driver retrieved their luggage from the trunk, collected his fare and drove away.

"You must be the Thomases," Walter said.

"Yes, Charles and Alice," replied the man.

"Walter Birkhoefer and my wife, Mary," Walter said by way of introduction.

"My, you have a lovely home," said Alice.

"Did you have a pleasant trip?" Walter asked.

"We came by bus. It was crowded and noisy. Charles can't drive long distances anymore, and we like to go someplace new when we take our annual vacation."

"Room five, Mary?"

"Yes."

"I'll take your bags up for you once you're registered. Mary will look after that." Walter motioned for the others to precede him inside. He prayed that Grace had a quiet night. He didn't think these people could cope.

It had taken some coercion, but he convinced his daughter to move into the room next to the one she'd used until now. Like the tower room, the room directly above the snug would be sealed off. The promise of ice cream with real maple syrup as a bedtime snack was the clincher. While this new room might not be larger than her old one, at least this one had normal corners. No crazy angles. And it had a fireplace. With Grace's blessings, he'd put Clara's new cradle by the hearth. Then she shushed him so that Clara could have her nap.

Mary registered her new arrivals. She couldn't ask for their car registration because they didn't come by car.

She left that blank and noted they arrived by taxi and the firm. There was only one in town, so it wouldn't be hard to track down the driver if needed.

Walter returned after taking the guests and luggage to their room. "They're going to join us in the snug for a pre-dinner drink. What are we having for supper tonight?"

Oh, Lord. Supper. With everything else going on, it had completely slipped her mind. Great hotelier she was. Mary dashed into the kitchen and opened the refrigerator door. Last night's leftover pot roast was there. What could she do with it? Meat pie. It wouldn't take long to roll out a couple of crusts. Add some flour to the gravy to thicken it. Boil some potatoes and come up with a vegetable; that would do. There was more apple pie, or at least there should be. She'd baked more than one the other day when she cooked for the reception. A quick check in the pie cupboard and there was the rest of the one they ate last night along with a full one. She breathed a sigh of relief. This was doable.

Mary returned to the snug. The Thomases had joined her husband. "I assume since you don't have a vehicle, you'll be dining with us this evening."

"If that's all right with you," Charles said.

"More than all right. We're having a beef pot pie, potatoes, yellow beans, and apple pie with either ice cream or cheddar cheese."

"Do we have lots of ice cream, dear? I promised Grace a bowl with maple syrup tonight before bed. I can go to the store if we need more."

"Perhaps you should."

After Walter left to go shopping for the ice cream, Mary left her guests alone and started preparing the crust for the beef pot pie she'd decided to make for supper. Once it was rolled out and into a plate, she put in the leftover roast with the carrots, potatoes and onions. The gravy had been in a separate bowl in the fridge, so she put it in a pot on the stove and warmed it. Then, added flour and stirred until it thickened. After it was poured over the contents in the pie plate, Mary put on the top crust and fluted the edges.

The rest of the meal preparation went quickly, and soon, a pot of potatoes and another of yellow beans were bubbling.

Mary turned down the heat under the pots and strode to the dining room, where she set the table for the couple. Walter would be back from the store soon, and if the Thomases were still in the snug, then he could entertain them.

It was a hit to say she winged it when she prepared the meal, especially with Mr. Thomas. He even requested a second helping of beef pot pie.

Chapter Twenty-One

After finishing their meal, the Thomases returned to their room. Alice retrieved her knitting from her bag and sat in the chair closest to the floor lamp. As she worked under the soft glow from the incandescent bulb, the room temperature suddenly chilled.

"Charles, would you close the window, please? I'm feeling the cold."

Her husband, who reclined on the bed, reading a novel, put it facedown and got up. "It's closed, Alice."

Why did the room go so cold? She wasn't prone to panic attacks or believing in the supernatural. Alice took a break from her needlework and went to the window. She pulled the curtains aside, and a young woman, maybe in her early twenties, dressed in a long white nightgown, walked across the lawn. Perhaps it was her going outside that caused the sudden drop in temperature. The room had warmed considerably in a short period.

Alice turned to her husband. "There must be someone else staying here. I saw a young woman in the grounds."

"That's nice, dear. Now, if you don't mind, I'd like to continue reading *The Murder of Roger Ackroyd* by Agatha Christie."

"Very well."

No sooner had she settled in and picked up her

knitting, a woman's voice became audible. It was soft but saddened by something. The tone was melancholy. It had to be the woman she saw outside. Her room must be next to theirs.

At about eleven o'clock, Alice put down her knitting and completed her bedtime ablutions. Her husband was still on the bed with his book when she slipped under the covers beside him.

Chapter Twenty-Two

AUGUST 3, 1914

This was the first day Patience left her bedroom. She had spent all her time sequestered in it, mourning the loss of her husband and stillborn granddaughter. Matilda and Catherine had tried to get her to eat something, but she refused. They even brought meals to her on trays. She still didn't want to eat, but staring at those same four walls was beginning to drive her crazy.

Bartholomew and Ophelia's bedroom was next to hers. She'd heard her daughter's gut-wrenching sobs on many occasions. Listening to the weeping broke Patience's heart, but she was also in mourning. The worst was when the undertaker arrived to take Anna's body away to prepare it for burial. Ophelia shrieked and cried, begging the man to give her daughter back to her. She wasn't nearly as upset when the police took her husband away to jail.

After she washed, Patience pulled out a black crepe gown. This was the first time she'd worn it since her arrival in Canada; she couldn't remember when she last wore it, only that it was back in England. She brought it with her, and never thought she'd need it so soon.

She crept down the stairs, hoping to avoid seeing anyone, but Matilda came out of the kitchen as she reached the living room door.

"Mrs. Kembleford. It's good to see you up and

about. Can I get you anything?"

"Coffee."

"Nothing to eat?"

"I'm not hungry."

"At least let me fix you a slice of toast. You need to eat to keep up your strength. Come and sit in the kitchen while I make it for you."

Patience complied. When Matilda made her mind up to do something, it was futile to disagree or resist. A few minutes later a buttered slice of golden brown toast, and a cup of coffee were placed at the table before her.

"Has Ophelia come down at all?"

"No, Mrs. Kembleford. Catherine has tried to get her to leave her room or the nursery but she insists on staying up there."

"I'll go speak to her later. And Lavinia? Where is she?"

"I believe she's gone for a walk."

Patience nibbled on the food. She hadn't eaten since breakfast on that fateful day. Her stomach cramped so after only a few bites, she put it down and drank the coffee. When she was done, she walked to the living room and sat down to write a letter to her mother.

3 August, 1914

Dearest Mother,

My life has taken the most awful turn. Not only have I lost Albert, but Ophelia's baby girl came early and was stillborn. Albert took his own life. All this happened on 31 July. Just mere days ago. In my last letter I mentioned my misgivings surrounding his recent behaviour. I'm starting to see why now.

The police and the Bailiff visited the lumber mill the other day. Albert had been embezzling funds from the business to keep up the payments on our home. He gambled away all of our savings. Our day-to-day living money, too. I'm not sure what we'll do. The foreclosure letter for the house and lumber mill was found in Albert's study. I can't believe he's gone. And Bartholomew,

Ophelia's husband, has been arrested. From what I can gather from the scant bits I've been told, he doctored the books so that the business finances looked in order.

My husband is dead. Ophelia's baby is dead. Lavinia is, well, she's not ... doesn't seem to be affected by any of it. I don't know if it's shock or she doesn't care. Doesn't grieve. My poor Ophelia, she's at her wit's end. Cries. Sobs, actually. She's not eating. It's as if she died along with her father and baby.

I don't know how much longer they'll let us stay in the house since it now belongs to the bank. I hope they give us some time to find a new home. It is just such a mess.

You didn't need to be burdened with this, but I thought you should know what's happened. I love you dearly and wish I hadn't had such bad news.
Your loving daughter,

Patience

Patience was in no fit state to take this to the post office. She addressed the envelope, put the letter inside and sealed it. She'd ask Matilda to send it. James. He needed to be told. She took out another sheet of paper and began to write.

3 August, 1914

Dear James,

I hate to be the bearer of such tragic news, but it's up to me. as they are your family. Your father is dead. He died on July 31. Ophelia's baby died, too, on the same day.

I hope Mr. and Mrs. O'Connor will find it in their hearts to let you come home for a short time in our time of need. I don't want to burden you anymore at this time; just know I love you.

Please come home. Your sisters and I need you.

Your loving mother

Patience rang the bell for the maid. She'd barely put it back on the desk and Matilda was there. "I need you to mail two letters for me. One to my mother in England, the other to my son. Please send them both first class. I'll compensate you for the postage when you return."

"Yes. Mrs. Kembleford. Right away, Mrs. Kembleford." The Maid of All Work took the two envelopes, put them in her apron pocket, and dashed out the door.

Chapter Twenty-Three

JULY 3, 1947

"Did you sleep well?" Mary asked her guests when she brought breakfast into the dining room.

"Very. The room was most comfortable except when it turned quite cold. I think it must have been the draft from a door opening and closing because it didn't last long," Alice said.

Mary hadn't gone outside last evening, nor had Walter. So whatever caused the drop in temperature wasn't down to what Mrs. Thomas said.

"I saw a woman out on the lawn last night. Do you have another guest staying here? Perhaps we'll meet her before breakfast is over."

No one else was booked in at the hotel. Not until the weekend. Had Mrs. Thomas seen a ghost? It sounded like the apparition that Grace referred to as 'that lady.' "What did this woman look like?"

"Long, dark hair. Come to think of it, I thought it was strange she was outside in her nightgown. Floor length, long sleeves, and high neck. Bare feet, too."

It was definitely 'that lady.' Mary had seen her the previous day when she had gone out to hang a load of laundry on the line. At least Mrs. Thomas wasn't frightened by the ghost — yet. She hoped it wouldn't come to that. "What are your plans for today?" she asked.

"Charles wants to go into Pike Falls, don't you,

dear? Have a wander and maybe a natter with the locals. We didn't really see much on the bus or in the cab on our way here. It's too bad your hotel is on the outskirts of the town. You'd do a booming trade if you were along the main road."

"There was a hotel there at one time. It burned to the ground in the spring of 1914, so we were told when we approached the council about converting the manor house into one."

"Interesting," mused Charles. "I don't suppose the town was nearly as big as it is now. The fire must have caused quite the commotion."

"No doubt," said Mary. "I'll let you folks eat now before it gets cold. Be careful; the plates are hot. I warmed them in the oven before I put your meals on them."

Mary found Walter puttering in the flowerbed outside the kitchen. "Mrs. Thomas had an encounter — not really an encounter — a sighting last night. She saw the ghost of Ophelia Kembleford in the front yard. Thought she was another guest. Don't let on any different to her. Unless something strange happens, and then we'll have to tell her. Oh, and I saw Ophelia's ghost yesterday when I hung out the washing. She was heading towards the boathouse."

"As long as there was no physical contact. I don't see it being a problem." Walter stood and stretched.

"They're going into town today."

"Why don't I drive them? It's a long walk for someone who isn't used to it and doesn't know the area. They can phone when they're ready to return and I'll pick them up. I'll just go tell them."

"I'm sure they'll appreciate it," Mary said. She turned around and went back inside.

Grace bounded into the kitchen, clutching Clara to her chest. That was a good sign. That, and no nightmares or ghostly encounters.

"You and Clara get up to the table, and I'll get your breakfast."

"Thank you, Mother. Come Clara. Into your

highchair."

Mary brought a bowl of cornflakes to the table and placed it in front of her daughter. The milk and sugar were already there, so she poured on the milk and then sprinkled sugar over the top. "Brush your teeth after you're done," she reminded.

"Yes, Mother."

Grace shovelled the cereal into her mouth. She attacked it like she hadn't eaten in at least a year. Mary reached for the coffee pot and poured herself another cup. She had a few moments to sit and relax before she had to clear away the Thomases breakfast dishes.

"My wife tells me you're planning on going into town today," Walter said when he entered the dining room.

"Why yes."

"I'll be happy to take you in my car. It's a long walk for someone who doesn't know the area."

"That's very kind of you. We'll accept your offer. You must tell your wife that breakfast was delicious," Alice said. She dabbed her mouth with the napkin, placed it on the table, and stood. "Come along, Charles. We don't want to keep the man waiting all day."

This was the way hotelier life was supposed to be. No ghostly apparitions, no attacks, no strange noises or smells. Guests enjoying their stay.

Walter returned from chauffeuring the Thomases into Pike Falls. He left them on the Main Street with strict instructions for them to call the hotel from the payphone at the bus depot when they were ready to come back, and he would pick them up. He even wrote the phone number down on the flap of a matchbook he found in the glove box.

He returned to the hotel content in his chosen profession. The night with the Rankin couple was a fluke. It had to be. Grace was over whatever had bothered her the previous few nights. Moving her into a different bedroom seemed to do it. He'd have to get to work and get that room sealed off. That would be today's job, made easier with their guests down in the town.

"I'm back, Mary," he announced when he entered the main hallway.

She entered from the dining room carrying a tray of dishes.

"You don't have to worry about making up the Thomases room. She told me that she made the bed and they'll use the same towels as yesterday. She said you looked tired and she didn't want to burden you."

"That was very kind of her." Mary disappeared into the kitchen.

"I'm going to seal up that bedroom today. Hopefully, that will put an end to the strange goings on," he called. "I'm going to see what supplies I have here, but I might have to get more."

The phone on the check-in desk rang. Mary rushed out of the kitchen to answer it. "Hello."

"It's Alice Thomas. We're going to stay in town longer and have a bite to eat at the diner. Tell your husband not to worry about coming to get us. We'll take a taxi back," she said.

"Are you sure?"

"Quite. I won't keep you. You'll pass that message along."

"Certainly."

Mary ended the call and went upstairs to pass the information on to Walter. By now, he had the door opening boarded up. They just needed to paint and paper. She'd seen wallpaper of this pattern in another room. It might not be the same colour because what was on the walls here in the corridor had most likely faded over the years.

For the night, Mary and Walter moved the mirrored hall stand in front of it. While she cooked and cleaned, he could paint and paper. She just had to remember where the bolt of wallpaper was.

Chapter Twenty-Four

During July, business at the hotel waned. Too many guests had strange experiences. None were ever as bad as their first customers, Doris and Bill Rankin. That couple fled before even spending the night. The Thomases stayed the two nights they had booked, and other than when Alice thought she saw another guest out on the lawn, and experienced the chill in their room, nothing else strange happened while they were in residence.

Word of mouth was a powerful thing. Mary thought that anyone who had a bad experience, whether ghostly or not, would tell people to avoid the hotel at all costs. Today, she had a group of six. All the rooms were made up, including the ones on the third floor under the eaves of the mansard roof. If any of them were close to six feet tall or over, she'd put them in the rooms on the second floor to give them the extra headroom, but if not, they drew the short straw or the low ceilings. They had only committed to the one night, but she had no other bookings, so if they decided to stay longer, they could. These people were the only guests she had booked thus far for the entire month.

They arrived in two cars. Four men and two women. Two of the men were shorter than the others, so they would be on the top floor with the female contingent of the party. The other two men would have rooms on the second floor.

"Welcome to the Kembleford Manor Hotel," she greeted them.

"Thank you," the shorter man said.

"Do you have any luggage?"

"We'll bring it in later once we're settled."

That seemed strange to Mary, but if they wanted to do that, she'd let them do it their way. She showed them the living room, dining room, and snug on the main floor, then escorted them to their rooms.

Grace played in her room with Clara as she walked by the open door. Finding the cradle in the tower room was a stroke of luck. Her daughter loved it, and she tucked Clara into it every afternoon for a nap and at night. Grace was growing into a big girl. She no longer had to sleep with her doll.

"Room five has a private bathroom accessed from within your room. Room six also has one, right here, just along the corridor from the room. You two gentlemen are here." She indicated to the taller ones. "You can choose which one you'd like. If the rest of you would follow me," she said, walking to the staircase to the topmost floor. "Unfortunately, there are no bathrooms on that level, but you can use the shower room next to the main stairs."

"Mind your heads on the sloped ceilings," Mary warned before she turned and went down to the main level.

"Do you think we should tell the landlady why we're here," Thelma asked the others assigned to the top floor.

"I don't think it's necessary," said Hazel. "If they think we're here for the occult, they might be less receptive to our presence."

"I agree with Hazel," said Roy.

Floyd nodded his head.

"I guess we should pick a room, then head downstairs and join Ernest and Stanley."

Once that was done, the four returned to the second floor, with Thelma bringing up the rear.

The door to the shower room Mary mentioned was open, as was the one that went with room six. She counted the other doors. Unless their hosts slept in separate bedrooms, one down here was unused.

The group made their way to the main staircase. "Do you hear that?" Hazel asked. Her eyes widened.

"What?" Stanley asked.

"Crying. Coming from there," she pointed to the room Walter had sealed off.

"There's nothing there. It's your imagination," said Ernest. "Come on, let's go downstairs."

Reluctantly, Hazel followed the others. She did hear crying coming from that part of the house. And she felt a definite chill in the air.

On the main level, they investigated the rooms they'd been told about earlier. The living room was too formal for Hazel's liking. It wasn't designed to be functional. It was all for show. The kind of space where you wouldn't want to spill something.

The dining room, while formal, left her feeling less uncomfortable.

"Great table for a séance," Roy said, smiling.

"Good thing there are six of us, or we'd never be able to hold hands around it," said Thelma. She passed her hand over the smooth surface of the mahogany piece.

So far, the only supernatural experience had been the crying from upstairs. This room, and the one they'd visited earlier, held no psychic vibrations. They visited the snug next.

The smell of cigar smoke tickled Thelma's nose. First, Hazel heard crying. Now, her and cigars. There was a presence in this room. "I think this is a far better room for a séance. There's a presence in here," she said, turning three-hundred and sixty degrees to take in the entire room. "We don't need a table. Move all the chairs into a circle unless you'd rather sit on the floor."

"Does anyone else smell cigars?" asked Floyd.

"You smell it, too?" Thelma replied.

He nodded.

"Gunpowder, too," Roy said. "Like someone fired a

gun in here." He sniffed the air as he walked around the room. "Stronger back here, closer to the windows."

"When do we want to hold the séance?"

"I think it's best if we wait until everyone is asleep. We can come down then and hold it. What do you think?" Stanley suggested.

"All in favour, raise your hands," said Thelma.

They all agreed to wait until everyone else had turned in for the night.

Shortly before midnight, Stanley led the group into the snug and closed the door behind them. He turned on the light once the door was closed so they could rearrange the chairs into a circle. Once everyone was seated, Stanley turned on his flashlight and extinguished the ceiling fixture. Then he set his torch light facing down on the floor, making an eerie glow around it.

"Join hands, everyone. Close your eyes, take a deep breath, hold it, and exhale. Rid your mind of all thoughts, open your eyes, and concentrate on the light in the centre of the circle. Picture us surrounded by this calming and pure light. Here, we acknowledge the presence of those who have come before us, the spirits that may join us tonight, and the divine forces that guide our journey," said Stanley.

"With the utmost respect, we invite positive and benevolent energies to surround us, offering their wisdom and guidance," Thelma continued. "Are there any spirits here tonight? If so, can you give us a sign?"

A strong breeze blew through the room. If a candle had been lit, it would have been blown out or tipped over and started a fire.

"Thank you, kind spirit. Can you manifest yourself so we might see you?" Stanley asked.

Nothing happened.

"Spirit, have we offended you?" Hazel asked.

Still nothing. Then, the room became cold. The temperature dropped about twenty degrees. The whiff of cigar smoke became more pronounced, and a haze filled the air.

"Kind spirit, was that another sign of your presence with us tonight?" Stanley asked.

"Can you tell us who you are?" asked Roy.

No response.

"I take it, spirit, that you lived in this house? Spent many hours in this room," said Hazel.

An audible sigh. It was as if the ghost was bored.

"I'm getting the sensation of extreme sadness and pain," said Thelma. "Would I be correct?"

The drapes on the window billowed like a breeze came through an open window.

"Spirit, is there another one like you here? In one of the rooms upstairs? Does this other spirit weep?" Hazel asked.

The light glowing out from beneath the flashlight brightened.

Stanley spoke again. "With gratitude and respect, kind spirit, we now close the gates between the seen and the unseen. May the energies joining us tonight return to their realms, and may our circle be safely closed. Let us take a few moments to ground ourselves. Feel the weight of your body on the chair, take deep breaths, and bring your awareness back to the room. As we conclude our séance, may the energy of this gathering continue to resonate within us. We release the protective energies that have surrounded us during this séance. May we move forward with open hearts and minds, knowing we are always guided and protected. As I turn off my flashlight, we symbolize the conclusion of our sacred gathering. May the light guide us on our individual journeys, and may we always be surrounded by love and positive energies."

After a few quiet moments, Stanley stood, walked to the switch, and turned on the ceiling light. The group stayed in the snug, discussed the séance, and speculated who the spirits might be.

"Let's call it a night. It's late, and we don't want to wake our hosts," said Stanley. Once the chairs were returned to their original positions and all six were next to the door, he turned the light out again, and they filed through. He closed the door quietly and followed the others.

Chapter Twenty-Five

When Hazel arrived in the dining room, the table had been laid for breakfast. She was the first member of the group downstairs. A coffee urn sat on the sideboard with cups, saucers, cream, and sugar. After last night, she needed a cup. She poured and breathed in the aroma as the hot liquid filled her cup. The others would be down soon. She'd heard them stirring when she descended the back stairs to the second floor.

This morning, no sounds of weeping came from the area where she had heard it the previous night.

One by one, the others entered and sat around the table. Their discussion returned to the events of last night. The séance, in particular. They stopped talking when Mary entered the room.

"Don't stop on my account. I just came in to take your breakfast orders. And I see you found the coffee all right."

Hazel's lips curled into a smile. "We were just talking about our plans for the day." It wasn't a total lie. Depending on how their chat went, it could mean them staying an additional day or more. "I don't suppose there's a place where we can get a newspaper?"

"If you don't care how recent it is, there are still extras from when we held our grand opening. It made the front page of the *Pike Falls Courier*."

Was there background information on the

property in the piece? If so, it might answer their questions from last night. "Perfect," said Hazel.

Mary left the room, reappeared a few minutes later with a copy of the paper, and handed it to the woman.

Hazel skimmed the article. There wasn't as much history as she had hoped. "Before these folks bought the place, it was the home of Albert Kembleford, a ruined lumber baron. That's the only mention of previous residents, although the piece ended ... 'When asked about the Kembleford Curse, Mr. Birkhoefer shook his head and laughed, saying he didn't believe in such things.'"

Mary returned with two plates of bacon, eggs and home fries. A little girl followed her. She carried a china doll under one arm and a ketchup bottle in her hand.

"What's your name, sweetheart?" Thelma asked.

"I'm Grace. I'm helping Mother today, but she won't let me carry the plates because I might drop them."

"I'm sure your mother appreciates your efforts." She turned her head towards where Mary stood, but the woman was gone.

She reappeared a couple of minutes later, and a man accompanied her. Between the two of them, they brought in the last four breakfasts. Walter introduced himself to the group.

"I was just reading the article on your grand opening. Very informative," said Hazel.

"Thank you. It's hard to believe that it was only a month ago, give or take a day or two, that we welcomed our first guests."

Mary nudged him. Thelma caught the subtle movement. His wife wanted him to stop talking. She managed to get him out of the room, but their daughter remained.

"What's your dollie's name?"

"Clara."

"That's a pretty name for a pretty doll. Where did you get her?"

"My grandmother," she said. "But 'that lady' says her name isn't Clara; it's Anna."

"Who's 'that lady'?"

"I don't know. But she's tried to take Clara from me. Said she wasn't mine. Told me she was hers and said her name was Anna."

Had this youngster had a ghostly encounter? The poor wee child.

"Off you go and help your mother, Grace," Thelma said.

The little girl skipped out of the room, clutching her doll.

Saturday. Would they be lucky enough that the newspaper offices would be open? They could go into town and check. If not, the town might have a library, and it could be open. Or, the librarian might know about the prior events in the house.

At breakfast, the men decided to do a little fishing, which meant Hazel and Thelma had the day to themselves. They returned to their rooms on the top floor. "Fancy a little shopping?" Hazel called from her room.

"I was thinking about what Grace told us and how the newspaper article ended. Why don't we see if we can solve that mystery first?" Thelma replied.

Hazel walked out into the corridor so she didn't have to yell again. "That's an excellent idea."

She returned to her room and grabbed her purse. It had the makings of a beautiful summer day. Blue sky. White, fluffy clouds. The temperature was in the mid-70s, so it wasn't too hot.

The two women exited the front door and turned toward the main street. Investigating first, shopping second. If they decided on staying another night, they'd have to ensure it was all right with their hosts. That depended on whether the men brought back any fish. And what they found.

The offices of the newspaper were closed. That was a huge disappointment. "Now what?" Hazel asked.

"Find out if the town has a library? Maybe they

keep copies of old newspapers there, or someone there will remember what happened and when."

"Let's try there." Hazel pointed to a diner across the street, and Thelma agreed.

They walked to the other side of the quiet road. Saturday in small-town Northern Ontario. No one was out and about. It was like the sidewalks had been rolled up. Things could become livelier later in the day.

Thelma opened the door and let her friend enter before her. A bell over the door tinkled.

"Take a seat. I'll be with you in a minute," a disembodied voice called from behind the counter.

"We don't want anything to eat or drink," Hazel said. "We wondered if Pike Falls has a library, and if so, where it is. We're staying at the Kembleford Manor Hotel."

"Don't get many requests like that in here." The waitress picked up a paper placemat printed with a map of the town. "We're here." She put an X on the map. "When you leave here, cross the street and turn to your left. The street out there is Front Street. The library is at the corner of it and Holditch Street." She drew another X there. "You'll be almost at the Pike River."

"Thank you. It sounds easy enough to find. Can we take this with us just in case?" Hazel asked.

"Sure. Have a nice day. Enjoy your stay in Pike Falls."

Thelma glanced at the map, checked for traffic, and then crossed the street with Hazel. Pike Falls was a lovely town. The buildings along this street were all in excellent repair. The sidewalks were clean. No rubbish blowing around. At least one garbage can was on every block; sometimes more. It depended on the distance between cross streets.

It only took them about five minutes to reach the square red-brick library. After they entered, the women walked directly to the counter where patrons returned or checked out books. The woman working the desk had a headful of curly grey hair and wore horn-rimmed glasses. If they were lucky, she lived in the area all her life and was definitely alive when all the disasters happened.

"Hello. My friend and I were wondering if you keep old issues of the *Pike Falls Courier* here," Thelma said.

"We do. What year are you looking for?" The woman stood.

"That's just it. We don't know. We're staying at the Kembleford Manor Hotel, and after reading the article on the grand opening, we were curious about the building's past," Thelma stated. "Especially the way that piece ended with the mention of the Kembleford Curse."

"I remember that article. Just last month. I attended the grand opening. I'd always been curious about the place and why it had lain empty for so long."

That might well be, but Thelma and Hazel wanted more information. "Apparently, it was the home of ruined lumber baron Albert Kembleford at some point." She couldn't say they held a séance there the previous night. The woman, Mrs. Crowell, according to her name tag, would think they were crazy.

"Follow me."

The librarian wasn't overly tall but rather stout and amply bosomed, unlike Thelma, who was slender and had no chest to speak of compared to her.

Thelma and Hazel were taken to a small room near the back of the building. They walked through tunnels between the shelves of books to get there. Inside, there was barely enough room for the three of them.

"The Kembleford Curse. I remember the reporter who coined the phrase. He ended up in hot water not too long after that. At least within a year or so." As Mrs. Crowell talked, she opened and closed drawers in a large cabinet. "Ah ha, here it is," she exclaimed, pulling it out of the drawer. "There's another one, too. Back then, the paper was only published once a week. Only recently did they start Monday to Friday. I think it was because of the war. People needed more information." Both papers were placed on the table for the women to peruse.

Thelma took a pen out of her purse and turned

over the placemat so she could write on it. Name, date, and cause of death. It tied in with their experience in the snug. His daughter was mentioned, as was the baby. One week later, the subsequent newspaper told the tragic tale of the premature infant.

"There should be one more. Early in the next year. I must have gone right by it." Mrs. Crowell returned the first two papers to their drawer and hunted for the other edition. "I was right. January 1915. Here you go, ladies."

"Ophelia Kembleford, also by suicide on December 31, 1914, on her sister's birthday," Thelma said as she copied the details.

"You mentioned, this reporter John L. Smith, ended up in trouble," Hazel said. "What sort of trouble?"

"I don't know if I should mention it with you both being ladies."

"We promise we won't be shocked. We come from a large city — Ottawa," said Thelma.

"Well," the librarian said, lowering her voice. "He took up with Miss Lavinia Kembleford and got her in the family way. The newspaper fired him when it came out. They both left Pike Falls. Poor Mrs. Kembleford ended up in an asylum. Nervous breakdown. No wonder, the poor dear."

"Thank you for your time and this information. You've answered all our questions and more."

Thelma and Hazel raced out of the library excited to share the news with their 'fisher' men.

"Do you think we'll be able to stay at the hotel for at least one more night?" Hazel asked as the women worked their way back along Front Street.

"I hope so. Now that we have this additional information, Stanley might want to lead another séance. Or let one of us do it."

"I wouldn't count on that. But at least last night, we all had the opportunity to ask questions. That doesn't happen often."

"Oh, look at that sweet dress in the window." Hazel stopped and admired the garment on the mannequin. The sign on the door indicated the store was open today, but it also said, 'Back in five minutes.'

"Yes, it is. I wonder what else the shop carries?" Thelma asked.

A few moments later, the sign on the door was removed, and the door unlocked. The women entered. The shop didn't appear to be very big from the street, but once inside, it opened up, and there was another level above. Hazel perused the dresses but couldn't find anything like the one in the window. What a disappointment. She preferred dresses to slacks.

Farther back in the store, men's clothing was displayed, and beyond that, a small housewares department. No sign of Thelma down here, so she must have gone upstairs. Hazel worked her way back through the store to the stairs. As she reached the top step, she saw Thelma.

The upper level of the Pike Falls Emporium held children's clothing and toys. Thelma turned at the footsteps drawing nearer. "What do you think, Hazel?" She held up a fancy doll costume. "It would be just about right for Grace's china doll."

"You hardly know the child. You only met her at breakfast. Why would you want to buy something for her or her toy?"

"Because I think she's a delightful little girl. Maybe a change in the outfit and the ghost won't believe that the doll is her daughter anymore."

"I think that's a bit much, but it is your money. I hope her parents let her accept the gift. And the dress in the downstairs window, I couldn't find any on the racks."

"That's too bad. I'll help you look before I pay for this. Maybe the store has more, but not in that colour? Two sets of eyes are better than one."

"That's true."

The friends returned to the lower level, searching for a dress like the one in the window. Their search was fruitless. "It might be the last one they have. Because it's on display, they might even give you a break in the price," said Thelma.

"That's all well and good, but if it isn't my size ..."

"There's the clerk. Go ask."

Hazel went off to speak with the employee. While she was gone, Thelma wandered through the racks of women's wear. She had plenty of clothes. Some might say, too many. Her late husband constantly complained about that. Nothing on offer appealed to her, so she walked to the cash register to pay for her purchase.

Hazel beamed. The shop had more of the dress she loved. They hadn't made it to the ladies' wear department yet. She tried one on in her regular size, and it fit. Perhaps she'd change into it when she returned to the hotel.

The two women left the store, carrying their purchases in brown paper bags with handles. "She didn't want to give us bags for our shopping," said Hazel.

"Small store, not long after the war, most locals likely have their own shopping bags. It's probably an expense the shops can't afford. They're rather sturdy, so I might use mine again until it wears out," Thelma replied.

"Good idea. I think I'll do the same."

Despite the huge breakfast, Hazel's stomach growled. "Oh dear."

"Do you want to stop in at the diner for a coffee and slice of pie?"

"Well, no. We must find the men and tell them what we found at the library. You haven't lost that paper, I hope."

"It's in my purse. Don't worry. The hardest part of all will be finding where they went fishing."

When they returned to the hotel, Thelma sought out Mary. She might know where the men were fishing. Her husband might have joined them.

"I'm not sure where they'd go. Did they bring their own fishing gear with them? If not, they'd have to go to the bait and tackle shop. It's back in town at Minnehaha

Bay. I don't have a map, or I could show you."

"I have one. I picked it up at the diner." Thelma dug in her purse and pulled out the placemat she'd written on. She laid it flat on the counter. Mary took a pen and marked the bay.

"The fishing is good in that area, I've been told. So your friends may have stayed around there."

Walking back into Pike Falls wasn't something Thelma wanted to do. The cars were still outside, so the men had to have walked. Staying put was the prudent thing to do. She and Hazel could walk back into town one way, and the men come back another, and they'd miss each other.

"I bought something for Grace's doll. I hope that's okay. I wanted to ask you first."

"You didn't have to do that."

"I know. I wanted to. This outfit told me it wanted to come with me because it knew a little girl who had a doll it would fit."

"I-I don't know what to say." Mary's face turned red, and she bowed her head. "Grace is playing in her room upstairs. I can call her down if you like."

"No. I'll stop in on my way to my room."

"Hello, Grace."

The little girl stopped what she was doing and turned towards the voice. "Hello."

"Can I come in?"

"Yes."

"I was in the Pike Falls Emporium this morning, and this told me it wanted to come home with me for your doll."

Grace jumped to her feet and took the bag from the woman's hand.

"I hope you like it," Thelma said as she squatted to get to the child's level.

The package inside was pulled out.

"Do you think it will fit her? I hope so because it's so pretty."

Grace picked up her china doll and held the outfit in front of her. "It will fit Clara."

161

"Would you like some help to get it out of the wrapping?"

"Okay."

Thelma unwrapped the dress and handed it to her. A bonnet came out next, and finally, socks and shoes.

The child stripped the doll of its current clothes. A white dress that could have been mistaken for a nightgown. Maybe that's why the ghost of Ophelia Kembleford was convinced Clara was her daughter, Anna.

This royal blue velvet, empire-waisted dress looked perfect on the doll. There was no reason for it to be confused with something of a similar size anymore.

Once Grace had Clara dressed in the complete outfit, Thelma tied the strings of the bonnet. The little girl threw her arms around Thelma's neck.

"Thank you," she said. "Clara says thank you, too."

"You and Clara are both most welcome. I'll let you go back to playing now."

Thelma stood and continued to her room on the floor above. She brought *The Uninvited* by Dorothy Macardle with her, so this afternoon was the perfect time to sit outside and read with a tall, cool glass of lemonade.

Thelma had no sooner settled into the lawn chair with her book and drink when the men returned. They didn't have any fish with them, so either they weren't biting today, or they had put them back for someone else to catch another day. "Any luck?"

"Ernie got one. A good-sized one, too, but the crafty bugger got off the hook at the last minute," said Floyd.

"Well there's always tomorrow. Hazel and I had a rather productive morning. Let me run upstairs and get my purse. Won't be a minute."

Thelma sprinted to the door. By the time she reached the bottom of the main staircase, she was out of breath. No way she could run up two sets of stairs.

Thelma climbed the rest of the way at a more sedate pace. When she passed Hazel's room, the door was open, and she was napping. Let her sleep.

She retrieved the placemat from the diner and returned to the garden where the men waited. "Okay, so this is what we found out." Thelma relayed the information she'd written down from the newspaper articles. And added the tidbit of gossip about Lavinia and the reporter who coined the phrase 'Kembleford Curse.' "Now that we know all this, I think we should stay another night and have another séance. We'd know for sure who the ghosts are. Or should."

"Could work," said Stanley.

"Can't see why not," added Roy.

"The worst that will happen is the spirits won't talk to us two nights in a row," said Floyd.

"You're awfully quiet, Ernie."

"Just thinking about the one that got away." He sighed and shoved his hands in his pockets.

Chapter Twenty-Six

AUGUST 3, 1947

The clock chimed midnight as Stanley led the others into the snug. The house had been quiet for an hour. With the added information the women got at the library, extending their stay and seeing what other phenomena they could discover made sense.

The Birkhoefers were thrilled to have them stay on. With their bookings dwindling, word of mouth from someone must have put non-ghost-hunting people off. He and his five friends benefitted from the lack of trade.

Chairs moved into position; everyone took their seats. Stanley waited by the door and turned out the light. Again, he used his flashlight on the floor as a candle, and they began. Stanley's introduction didn't vary from the one he used their first night in the hotel.

"Have any spirits associated with Kembleford Manor joined us this evening?" Hazel asked. "If so, could you give us a sign?"

Nothing happened immediately, but the cigar smell and smokey haze soon filled the room.

"Kind spirit, in life, were you Albert Kembleford?" Stanley asked.

"We've seen the newspapers from 1914," Thelma said. "We know how you died. Does it grieve you, kind spirit, to be at unrest?"

The smell and smokiness dissipated.

"Is your daughter, Ophelia, with you tonight? And her daughter, Anna?" Hazel asked.

"You never knew you were almost a grandfather," said Ernest.

"That was unnecessary," Stanley said.

"Kind spirit, is it Ophelia who people have heard crying?" Floyd asked.

That was the first time he actively participated in one of their séances in a long while. Stanley nodded.

The glow from the upside-down flashlight intensified.

"Ophelia Kembleford, are you with us tonight?" Roy asked.

A woman's crying became audible and increased in volume.

"We know about your baby, and we're so very sorry for your loss," said Thelma.

The weeping grew fainter.

Tonight, two ghosts haunting Kembleford Manor were identified. Were there others? "Kind spirit, we know of you and your daughter who still roam the rooms and corridors of this great house. Are there any other spirits here? Spirits from a time before you?" Ernest asked.

Nothing.

At least tonight, Ernie contributed something useful after his comment about not knowing about the granddaughter. Stanley concluded the séance. The six rehashed the events. "I would take it from the lack of response to your question that there are only the two spirits here."

"Agreed," said Thelma. "And we now know for sure who 'that lady' Grace has had encounters with is."

"Let's put this room back in order, and we'll go to bed. I, for one, can't wait to get stuck into another of Mary's breakfasts. She is an excellent cook," Stanley said.

"And no mention to the family about the séance and that we know the hotel is haunted. We might not be welcome to extend our stay otherwise," said Hazel.

Ernest paused in front of the coffee urn set up in the same place this morning on the dining room sideboard. His mind drifted back to the fish that got away. It was either an enormous pike or a smaller muskie. He might try again to catch him, but there were no guarantees of success. The crafty creature was probably long gone from the area they had fished the previous day. No sense crying over it, he filled a mug with the rich, dark, steaming liquid.

As he sat at the table, he mused over the séance. Stanley went a bit overboard at his comment about Albert Kembleford being dead before finding out he was going to be a grandfather. As it turned out, it wasn't meant to be.

The smells of breakfast cooking wafted into the dining room. Ernie perked up and sniffed the air. Bacon. Crispy and not greasy. The woman must de-grease it somehow. On a paper bag?

About eight o'clock, the others joined him.

"You're not still moaning about yesterday and losing that fish, are you?" Roy asked.

"No," said Ernest. "If you must know, I'm fantasizing about breakfast."

"Mrs. Birkhoefer is an excellent cook," said Thelma, serving herself a mug of coffee.

"Agreed," Stanley said.

"What plans do we have for today?" Hazel asked.

Ernest was easygoing, and unless their plans were repulsive, he went along with them.

Thelma carried her filled mug to the table and sat beside Floyd. Stanley, as usual, sat at the head of the table. Most days, she found him overbearing and arrogant, but he was an excellent séance leader, so she tolerated his lesser-liked character traits.

"I assumed everyone would want the same again this morning, so I went ahead and cooked it," said Mary when she entered the room. "There are also sausages if anyone would like them, too."

"I wouldn't say no to a couple," said Roy.

"In addition or instead of bacon?"

"Addition, please."

Mary left the room once everyone advised her of their choice. Thelma was the only member of the group who kept the same options as the previous day.

From her seat at the table, she couldn't see the hallway. She overlooked the bay window and the scenery beyond. The heavy drapes were wide open and tied back. A large black crow perched on the hotel sign. Soon, another joined it. Thelma found it amusing when birds this size hopped. Little birds like chickadees and sparrows, it seemed normal. But crows?

Grace was with Mary when the woman returned with the breakfasts. Today, she pushed a cart with a large tray on it. Clutched in Grace's arm was the china doll still dressed in the outfit Thelma bought the day before. "Clara must really like that dress. She's still wearing it," Thelma said.

"I like it, too. Clara doesn't look like an Anna now." She held the doll out from her body towards the table and smiled.

A few seconds later, the little girl frowned.

"What's wrong, Grace?" Thelma asked.

"'That lady.' She's behind you. She looks angry."

Ophelia Kembleford's ghost in the dining room. Before she turned around, Thelma asked the others if they saw the apparition. Only Stanley and Ernie saw it. Or at least they were the only two who admitted it.

By now, Thelma was turned around in her chair. The translucent figure of Ophelia Kembleford floated about three inches off the floor behind her. In life she had been an attractive woman with long dark brown hair. In death, her once beautiful features were distorted. Her eyes were bugged out, and surrounded by dark circles, and her head tipped towards her shoulder. Rope burns surrounded her neck.

Thelma moved slowly to her feet and then stood with her back to the table. "Hello, Ophelia. How can we help you this morning?"

The spirit remained silent.

There had to be a reason for the sudden manifestation.

"Anna," the spectre whispered.

"Where is Anna?" Thelma asked.

"In that child's arms." This time, the voice was louder, and the words spat out in anger.

Risky or not, it was one Thelma was willing to take. "That's not Anna in Grace's arms. That's her china doll, Clara."

"Anna!"

Thelma refused to be dragged into an argument with the ghost. She turned her back on it and returned to her chair. "Has she gone now?"

"Y-yes," Grace said.

"Are you all right, sweetie?"

The little girl didn't answer; she just bolted from the room.

"Well, that was interesting," Stanley said. "Two séances here and no manifestations of the spirits that haunt this place, and here at breakfast, we're joined by one of them." He stabbed a sausage with his fork, cut it and shovelled it into his mouth.

Someone in the house or their group had to be a medium. He wasn't. Maybe one of the women? If so, it was most likely Thelma since the spirit chose her chair to stand behind. If the ghost of Ophelia Kembleford couldn't tell the difference between a baby and a china doll, then she must be crazy. Insanity might have run in the family. But then, losing your father and your baby the same day and your husband being sent to prison could be what tipped her over the edge. Symbolic that she hanged herself on her sister's birthday. Perhaps an act of revenge? Bad feelings between the siblings over a man? Not just any man, but Ophelia's husband? He decided it wasn't worth the speculation.

Chapter Twenty-Seven

AUGUST 31, 1947

Mary went about her daily routine. After a few weeks, with Mrs. Pritchard's help and the sudden lack of patronage for their hotel, she could keep up with running the house and cleaning the guest bedrooms when required. Walter had sealed the tower thoroughly from both front bedrooms, so you couldn't open the secret panel unless you knew where the button was. He had even sealed off the small bedroom above the snug. It had been the source of their daughter's night terrors and other ghostly encounters. Still, there were times when Mary walked by the room when she heard a woman's voice singing or humming a lullaby or a woman crying.

This ghost, which manifested when the mood suited, was the only one she had encountered since they moved into Kembleford Manor. The occasional whiff of cigar smoke meant another being was about, but the smoker never approached or attacked the family. If Mary didn't know better, she'd swear the spirit of Ophelia Kembleford liked to terrorize for the sheer pleasure of it. And it seemed poor Grace and her china doll, Clara, bore the brunt of the dead woman's torment.

Mary walked to the back door to call Grace in for lunch. She'd been playing on the swing Walter had hung from one of the large maple trees the last time she saw her daughter. With no sign of her, Mary went outside. Her husband was weeding one of the flowerbeds back here. "Have you seen Grace," she asked.

"Is she not with you?"

"No. She was out here swinging. You know how she loves to do that."

"I don't think she's too far away." Walter stood and brushed off the front of his trousers. "I'll go look for her."

"I'm coming with you." This disappearance was out of character for their daughter. She always stayed where she said she'd be. If not, then she'd come and say something.

Mary and Walter started their search in the hotel. Every room. Under every bed. Walter even checked the secret panel to the anteroom and the tower with no sign of her.

"She wouldn't go off on her own. Not unless ...

"Unless what, dear?"

"She was lured." Tears pricked Mary's eyes. She didn't want to cry, but she had no control and didn't know where Grace was and if she was safe. When they started, the floodgates opened. Hot, scorching tears tumbled down Mary's cheeks.

Walter encircled her with his arms in an attempt to comfort her, but it was to no avail. "There's no one around here who would do such a thing. Pike Falls is a safe community."

"What about the ghost of Ophelia Kembleford? You know she's had it in for Grace since day one."

"Don't talk such nonsense, my dear. Why don't I make a call to Mrs. Pritchard? Maybe she went over there."

Mary clung to her husband as they made their way into the house and the telephone at the reception desk. Walter placed the call. He was only on the phone for a minute.

"Thank you. Sorry to bother you," he said, placing the receiver on the cradle. "Grace didn't go there, so she must be here somewhere. Let's search the grounds."

Walter led the way out the front door, and they began their search at the circular driveway and the parking area on this side of the property. No sign of the little girl. Both he and his wife called out her name but didn't receive a reply. He began to worry.

He started in the direction of the boathouse. Walter was about halfway across the property when he broke into a run. It was the only place they wouldn't look for her. Grace had been forbidden to go near the building because it was old and unsafe. He flung open the side door. The sight before him turned his blood cold.

Floating face-down on the water was his daughter. His beautiful seven-year-old daughter. Next to her was Clara. Not taking time to remove his shoes, he leapt into the water. Two strides, and he reached her and rolled her onto her back. Was it too late? Walter lifted her into his arms and carried her to the dock. He patted her cheeks. "Grace, it's Daddy. Wake up, sweetheart."

Grace didn't respond. He tried again, but it was less gentle this time. Still no response. He didn't know how to do artificial respiration. He couldn't save his little girl.

Mary heard the splash and ran to the boathouse. She dropped to her knees and pulled Grace to her bosom. Walter had his back to her, his head bowed. It was too late. If only she'd looked for her sooner. Maybe she wouldn't be gone now. How could she live with herself knowing that it was her fault her daughter was dead.

"If only I knew what to do. I might have been able to save our sweet child," Walter lamented.

"You're not the one to blame. If I'd looked for her sooner, I might have been able to prevent Grace from coming to this awful building in the first place. We were so concerned with making the house a safe place that we never gave the boathouse a second thought. We'd forbidden her to go near it. We should have done more. Padlocked the door or something." Mary's tears flowed again. "Fish Clara out of the water. Grace will want her with her."

The sadness inside Mary turned to anger. "It's

that ghost of Ophelia Kembleford behind this. I know it is. You've seen some of the things she's done to Grace. She was a lunatic when she was alive, and she's still one in death. If she wasn't already dead, I'd kill her myself with my bare hands. I hope you're happy now, you crazy … I can't say what I want to call you."

"Oh, my goodness. What on earth has happened?" Mrs. Pritchard squatted beside Mary. "After Walter telephoned me, I thought I'd come and help you both look for little Grace."

"I found her floating face-down in the water," Walter said.

"Let's get you into the house and out of those wet things. Even though it's summer, you'll still catch your death if you stay in them too long. Let me take the wee girl."

"No," Mary shouted.

"Well, at least let Walter carry her."

Mary relented and allowed her husband to scoop Grace up into his arms. She picked up Clara and clutched the doll to her chest.

Mrs. Pritchard stewed and fretted all the way back to the hotel. Grace had never mentioned anything about the boathouse to her since the family moved into Kembleford Manor. The little girl had been forbidden to go near it because it was unsafe. The child didn't know how to swim either. Would that have made a difference?

Was it the ghost of Ophelia Kembleford? Had she tossed Clara into the water, and Grace jumped in to save her, but the water was too deep? Or was it less sinister? The china doll fell into the water accidentally. No matter the cause of Grace's death, it was tragic.

The woman followed Walter and Mary up the stairs to the bedroom, where he laid Grace's body on her back on the bed, with Clara in her arms on her chest. His shoulders shook as he wept. Mary tried to comfort him, but she could barely hold herself up.

Mrs. Pritchard slipped out of the room. At the reception desk, she stopped and called the police station to report the drowning. Should she contact the only funeral home here in Pike Falls? Was that sticking her nose in too far? The Birkhoefers might have wanted to bury her in the village they moved away from. Still, the body would have to be transported there. She'd back off, and maybe the police would look after that aspect.

Tea. Hot, sweet tea was what Walter and Mary needed. The woman entered the kitchen, filled the kettle and put it on to boil. While waiting, she filled the cream pitcher, added cubes to the sugar bowl, and placed those items on the tray with cups and saucers. She spooned loose-leaf tea into the bottom of the teapot and, when the kettle boiled, poured in the hot water.

As she reached the turn to the stairs, the police pulled up out front. She walked to reception to wait for them. It was Chief Berwick himself and one of the constables she didn't know who entered the hotel.

"Follow me. I'm just taking the Birkhoefers some tea. Hot and sweet for the shock."

The three ascended the staircase and strode to the bedroom. Mrs. Pritchard put the tray on the dresser and backed out of the room. They didn't need her there.

Chapter Twenty-Eight

T wo days later, the newspaper carried the story of Grace's death. James Clancy was pleased with his piece, although he would have liked to get comments from the child's family. Still, it would generate interest in the strange happenings and tragedies at Kembleford Manor throughout the community. And that was what sold newspapers and kept him in a job.

Perhaps a trip to the Courier's archives would shed more light on events of the past. He'd go down into the basement where they were stored and have a look through past issues and previous reporters' stories. If he was fortunate, maybe their notebooks would be there, too. Unfortunately, no one who worked at the paper in 1914 when the shit hit the fan was still there. He doubted if any of them were still alive. The newspaper had been privately owned by the Selfridge family, but whether it had been passed down through the generations or sold off to someone else, he didn't know.

He stubbed out his cigarette in the ashtray and made his way down into the bowels of the building in search of more information.

The basement was cool and damp. There were better conditions for storing important documents. He found the files for 1914 and flipped through the folders to see if there was a specific one for Kembleford Manor or Kembleford Lumber Mill. Back then, the paper was only published one day a week, so there weren't a lot of documents to go through, but he came out empty-handed. James Clancy kicked the cabinet in frustration and stomped back up the stairs.

Back at his desk, he lit another cigarette and then re-read the piece he'd written. He got the information from somewhere. How else would he have known about the events in 1914? The top of his desk was a disaster waiting to happen. Papers and file folders, notebooks and pencils. He started tidying and found the source of the information he quoted. It came from the notepad of the reporter from back then. Did nothing else happen at Kembleford Manor before or after that year which warranted news coverage?

James went through the old notebook. There weren't many pages. This guy had a shorthand of his own, making the book hard to decipher. At least the dates were written in proper form. The biggest news in this former reporter's notebook was the fire that burned down the town's only hotel in the spring of that year.

At least now, he had a name. John L. Smith. He'd return to the archives and see if more of the man's notes existed. But not today. It was quitting time. He picked up his cigarette and left the office for home.

Chapter Twenty-Nine

SEPTEMBER 3, 1947

Back at the paper the following day, James returned to the archives in search of more notes from John L. Smith, but there were none. Maybe when the man retired, he took his notebooks with him. But why leave that particular one at the office? What did the others hold — if there were others — that maybe he didn't want anyone else to know about?

Was the man still alive? If so, he'd be pretty old and maybe not in possession of all his faculties. Would he even agree to meet with him?

There was only one cemetery and one funeral director in town. He'd start there. The weather that day was favourable, so he wandered through the graveyard first, searching for a headstone bearing the name John L. Smith. Unless there was no stone, he wasn't there.

On his way back to the office, he stopped at the funeral home. "James Clancy, *Pike Falls Courier*," he said, introducing himself.

"We know who you are. Trying to get some scoop on the Birkhoefer girl's funeral arrangements?"

"No, actually. I'm trying to find a John L. Smith who worked for the newspaper back in 1914. He covered the Kembleford Manor scandals. I wondered if you had a record from conducting his funeral?"

"I really can't divulge that information."

"Look, I just want to know if he's dead or alive. If it's the latter, I'll get the operator to put me through to

176

his house."

"I can tell you we've had no one here by that name, so I think you should leave." The funeral director ushered the reporter towards the door. "Wait, I remember the Kembleford Manor scandals. The son-in-law went to jail. We looked after the arrangements for Mr. Kembleford, his granddaughter, and his daughter the following year. But there were two other children. A son who moved away before all that happened. And another daughter."

James Clancy's ears pricked at the words. Was there more?

"Yes, I remember now. The youngest daughter, Lavinia, it was. She took up with this Mr. Smith you're looking for. The newspaper fired him. She ended up in the family way, thanks to him. They both left Pike Falls. Whether together or not, I can't say. I don't know if he did the decent thing and married the poor girl. I think the mother is still here somewhere in Pike Falls. But you won't get anything from her. She ended up in an asylum not long after. The poor woman."

He could track down some of the older residents and talk to them. It would be a start. But only if they lived in Pike Falls back when it all happened. "Thanks for the information. It's been a great help." He shook the man's hand and left.

The first thing he would do was go back to the archives and search after 1914 to see if there was any mention of this gold nugget the funeral director gave him.

Much to his chagrin, James Clancy found nothing in the archives. It was possible that at the time of the scandal, Mrs. Kembleford was still in possession of all her faculties and prevented the paper from printing anything about it.

Not that the current occupants would know that part of the history, he decided to drive to the Kembleford Manor Hotel. Maybe there were documents there? Yes, it was only a few short days after the drowning of Grace Birkhoefer, but what he sought might be in an outbuilding. The day of the grand opening, he'd spotted a couple of decent-sized sheds on the property. Not to mention the boathouse where the little girl drowned.

James tucked his package of cigarettes in his shirt pocket, grabbed his jacket off the back of his chair and set out. He quickly turned around. A camera. If he had a camera with him, he could photograph any evidence that supported the information the funeral director told him. If at all possible, he wouldn't bother the grieving family. Conduct his search, take pictures and leave. The newspaper office had its own darkroom, so he could get the young person who worked there to develop the film.

The first shed he searched on the Birkhoefer's property was filled with gardening tools, fertilizer, weed killer and a few containers he couldn't identify. Waste of time. He moved on to another outbuilding on the opposite side of the property. It was locked. That would be his luck. All the juicy details were boxed up in a building he couldn't access. Damn. So close. This shed was in line with the windows of the rooms the Birkhoefers used for themselves. He couldn't take the chance they'd see him if he was to try to jimmy the lock. If he were to come back at night with bolt cutters to remove the padlock, he'd need to bring a flashlight and attract unwanted attention.

For now, he'd check the boathouse. James crept towards the river, trying to stick close to the tree line so no one would see him. It worked. The door creaked when he opened it. Light filtered through from a hole in the roof. Some from under the door. No boats. Just docks around the edges and one up the middle. Room for two watercraft. Did the Kemblefords have any? Or was it the person they bought the property from? Having a boathouse and no boats didn't make any sense to him.

After a fruitless search, he came away disappointed and empty-handed. It was darker now. Time folks would be turning their indoor lights on. The manor house was in total darkness. James made his way back around to the other side of the property and peered in the windows of the Birkhoefers' personal living space. Empty. Not a stick of furniture. He checked the other rooms. Furniture that came with the house remained. Mary and Walter Birkhoefer had picked up stakes and moved on. Who could blame them?

Chapter Thirty

OCTOBER 16, 2022

After only a few hours of sleep, Nicole rose, showered, dressed, and grabbed her car keys. She never gave a moment of thought whether her brothers would be up or not. A few minutes later, she pulled her compact Chevy up to the curb in front of their apartment building. Her sketches from Kembleford Manor were what was necessary at the moment. The boxes of papers back at her apartment would wait. If they didn't hold anything else more interesting, she might bin them herself.

She pressed the intercom buzzer. When there was no reply, Nicole pressed it again. She danced from one foot to the other, willing one of her brothers to answer. Her wish finally came true when a groggy voice picked up.

"Hello?"

"Cooper, it's me. Let me in. I need my sketchbook."

A loud buzz resounded through the building's vestibule when he pressed the button to unlock the security door. Nicole wasted no time, yanked the door open and darted up the stairs to Cooper's apartment. The door opened as she reached the landing, and a bleary-eyed Cooper clad in flannel sleep pants stood in the opening.

"Nice to see you, too, sis," he said. "Do you have any idea what time it is?"

"Yes, I do. It's time you were out of bed. I've been up for hours. I wanted to compare my sketches with the SD card in my camera, but I couldn't since the drawings were here. I did get through one of the boxes of Mummy's stuff. I think it was her mother's. Old magazines, newspaper clippings from mostly in the 60s, some from before Mummy was even born, and some Canadian centennial money. I'm not sure what I'm going to do with it. Some of those things might be worth something to a collector. I don't know."

"Well, don't do anything rash. Maybe talk to Dad about some of that stuff. He might know how it came into Ma's possession. Want a coffee while you're here?"

"Love one." Nicole went straight to the living room and picked up her sketchbook from the coffee table.

"Hi, sis," Connor said as he passed from the second bedroom to the bathroom.

"Cooper's got the coffee on."

"Great, I could use one."

Nicole opened her sketchbook and leafed through the pages of drawings. When she got to the one of the drowned child and doll, she gasped.

Now wearing an Aerosmith T-shirt, Cooper sat a mug of dark roast on the table before his sister. "I have a confession to make. I looked at your sketches last night. I hope you don't mind."

"Well ... no, you're fine. We were all at Kembleford Manor, although when you and Connor went to the lumber mill, Mitch and I went to the boathouse."

"Is that where you saw the body floating in the water?"

"Yes. It was quite disturbing. It was a young girl. Maybe eight or nine at the most. And her doll."

"Hey, go back. The one with the woman in the window."

Nicole leafed back through the pages until she found the page Cooper had asked to see. By now, Connor was there as well.

"She looks like. You know. Her who played Queen Victoria in that PBS series. You know," Connor said.

"They say everyone has a doppelgänger," Nicole

said, closing the book.

"That's creepy." Connor sipped his coffee.

Nicole couldn't wait to get home and compare the photos she had taken while exploring Kembleford Manor with the sketches she had done. She bounded up the three flights of stairs. Once inside her apartment, she removed the SD card from her camera and put it into the slot on her laptop. At least the screen on her computer was bigger than the one on her camera. And if she still needed it to be larger, she had a USB card reader she could plug into the port on her 42-inch television.

She started viewing the images. Rooms where she'd seen nothing, as evidenced by her sketches, had strange orbs of light in the photograph. Others showed a blurry section somewhere in the picture. It was like her lens had a fingerprint on it. But she knew that wasn't the case. She continued.

When she got to the sketch of the woman, she believed to be Ophelia Kembleford holding her dead baby in the room over the home office, she paused looking at photos and googled the PBS series Victoria and found the name of the actress. She fired off a quick text to Connor.

Jenna Coleman

A few seconds later, the dancing dots appeared on her screen, so she knew he was replying.

Huh?

She loved her brother, but sometimes he had a memory like a sieve. It wasn't half an hour ago she was at the apartment he and his brother shared.

She played Queen Victoria on the PBS series.

At least they had one mystery solved. Nicole continued comparing her sketches to her photos. In some rooms where she'd sketched the strange phenomena in the room, her photos didn't show it. It could have been the delay between drawing and taking the picture that caused them not to show up.

She wished she had a better printer to capture these strange images. There were a few DIY photo machines in the area where she could take her card and

get prints, but they were limited to a specific size, like 4"
x 6." Ideally, Nicole would like these to be at least 8" x
10" or larger.

The sketch in the boathouse brought a tear to her
eye. She didn't know who the little girl was. Or how she
came to be in the water. When she clicked through to
view the next image on her screen, it was the same. She
didn't take a photo. Seeing the drowned child was so
much of a shock. Maybe Mitch grabbed her camera? He
claimed he didn't see anything in there. And he would
have had to taken the strap from around her neck. She
pulled out her phone, looked up Mitch in her contacts,
and tapped out a text to him.

Did you take a picture at the boathouse?

About fifteen minutes later, she received his
reply.

No. Why?

There's one on my camera's SD card.

The dancing dots started and stopped a few times
before she received Mitch's reply.

Weird.

It was definitely that. Nicole needed to find out
who the child was who drowned. There was no
indication of the year the tragedy happened.

N, coming over. Have to see it for myself.

Nicole opened the browser on her laptop and
typed drowning at Kembleford Manor into the search
bar. In no time, a page of results popped up on her
screen. Now that she'd minimized her photo viewer, she
hoped the image didn't vanish. Bizarre things happened
when they explored the mansion and the property.

About twenty minutes later, her doorbell rang.
Mitch had arrived so she buzzed him in, opened the
apartment door, and returned to her computer.

"Hey, Nicki, where are you?" he asked as he
entered her flat.

"In here." She brought up the photo viewing
software window, and the image was still there. A
massive sigh of relief escaped.

By now, Mitch had worked his way to the dining
room. "Well?"

"Pull the chair around and sit down."

When he did, Nicole turned the laptop to make it easier for him to see the screen. "Here it is. I know I didn't take it. I was too upset seeing that little girl face-down in the water. I remember the sketch I made. But this was *not* taken by me."

"I didn't take it either. Was it supposed to be a clue for you so you could find out the kid's identity?"

"I googled drowning at Kembleford Manor and got a bunch of hits. Here, look." She brought up the browser again.

"Try that one. It's the newspaper. With any luck, all their articles are online, and we can read them."

Nicole clicked on the link, and the newspaper's front page filled her screen. She scanned it quickly.

PIKE FALLS COURIER

Vol. 47167   Tuesday, September 2, 1947   One nickel

TRAGEDY STRIKES YET AGAIN AT KEMBLEFORD MANOR

James Clancy, Staff Reporter

On August 31, the body of seven-year-old Grace Birkhoefer was found drowned in the boathouse on the Kembleford Manor Hotel property. It is unknown how long she had been in the water when her body was discovered by her father, Walter Birkhoefer.

The mansion has seen its share of tragedies over the years. Back in the summer of 1914, it was home to two deaths. Albert Kembleford and his stillborn granddaughter, Anna Randall, both on July 31, followed later in the year by the death of his daughter, Ophelia, on New Year's Eve. Albert's death was a self-inflicted gunshot wound. His daughter hanged herself in the tower of the mansion. Coincidentally, her death fell on her younger sister's birthday.

Could it be the Kembleford Curse has reared its ugly head again?

At this time, funeral arrangements are unknown. The Birkhoefers are in seclusion, mourning the death of their only child.

"Those poor parents. Imagine what they must have gone through." A tear spilled down her cheek, and she dashed it away before Mitch saw it.

Guys, emailing you a link. You've got to see it.

She opened her email and sent the link to the article to both of her brothers.

She didn't know if they would open their emails as soon as they received them. She hoped they would. About ten minutes later, she had a reply to her text from Cooper.

Wow!

Short, sweet and to the point. That was Cooper.

A short time later, Connor responded.

That was the kid you saw in your vision? Creepy.

Nicole picked up her sketchbook and brought up the photo viewer again. Something needed to be added to the article. The doll. The china head doll wasn't mentioned. Was that the cause of the little girl's drowning? She dropped her toy, and when she went to retrieve it, she fell in and couldn't get out?

By now, she'd been through every sketch she'd done at Kembleford Manor, but the photo viewer showed still more pictures. Nicole clicked the mouse button. These were the photos she took in the tower of the engraving on the pieces of silver.

She opened a new tab on her browser and searched 'English silversmith with the initials PS.' That didn't bring up quite what she wanted, so she added the phrase 'in the 1800s.' This time, she got a Wikipedia article as the top site. Nicole clicked on the link and skimmed the article. Farther down the page, a photo of the underside of one of his pieces showed his stamp. She clicked on the image and brought it up to the full-screen size. Split screen images didn't work well on her laptop, so Nicole sent the photo she took to her phone so she could examine it and the marks on the website and compare the two.

"Look, Mitch, they're identical. First his initials,

then the lion, a shield, the letter u, and I think the last mark is a person wearing a crown."

"Sure looks like it."

"The silver in the trunk in the tower room at Kembleford Manor was Paul Storr. It would be worth a fortune today."

"Surprised that stuff was still up there," he said. "After all, another family lived there in the 1940s after the war. You would have thought they would have taken it when they moved out."

"Not necessarily." Nicki pulled her hair into a ponytail and secured it with the elastic she wore on her wrist. "It's possible they never went up into the tower."

"Yeah, I guess. I mean, it was barricaded."

"Maybe they're the ones who blocked the access. Those stairs could be dangerous. Maybe they had the room closed off to keep their little girl safe? Fat lot of good that did them. In the end, she drowned." Nicole rubbed her eyes.

"Hey, don't let it get to you. It happened long before our time. There's nothing you could have done to prevent it."

"I know." Nicole stood and stretched. "I need a coffee. Want one?"

"If you're buying."

"You'll have to settle for homebrew, but it's made in a French press. Come on, I'll show you."

The two entered Nicole's galley kitchen, and she prepared the coffee. Doing something other than being bent over the computer, staring between its screen and her sketchbook, had made her tired, and her eyes ached. It might not have been so bad, but she left her computer glasses at the office when she left work for the week. Usually, she didn't spend much time on her computer throughout the weekend. But then, this particular weekend wasn't exactly typical.

The two leaned against the counters and chatted, one on each side of the room so they faced each other. Just small talk and nothing about Kembleford Manor. Mostly other abandoned places they had explored, how their jobs were going. Plans for future explorations.

"You never did tell me how you came to be at Kembleford Manor yesterday," Nicole said.

"I've been exploring abandoned hotels. This one came up. I'd checked out the Paisley Inn last year. Before that, the Grand River Hotel, the Longbranch Motel. You guys tend to stick more to houses, some of which are fairly new builds, abandoned because the property has been sold to developers and it's waiting for demo, and older places. It was nothing more than a coincidence we ended up at the same place at the same time."

Mitch looked at his watch. "Is that time? I best get off. Things to do. People to see."

"I believe you where thousands wouldn't."

He drank the rest of his coffee, put the empty mug in the sink, and leaned down to kiss Nicole on the cheek. "See you. Let me know if you find more interesting stuff in those boxes."

"I will." She walked him to the door and saw him to the security door on her floor.

Mitch pondered the image of the drowned child that found its way onto Nicole's camera. He couldn't explain how it got there since he didn't take the photo, and Nicki swore she didn't. With how upset she was when she saw the ghostly drowning victim, she could have done it and then blocked it from her mind.

He unlocked his pickup truck and eased in behind the wheel. Mitch glanced towards Nicole's apartment, started the engine and drove off.

At one time, he and the Holbrook brothers explored many places together. Cooper was a control freak at times, but they always got along fine. What changed? He still got along with Connor. It was just Cooper who had a problem.

When they went their separate ways, Mitch turned his sights to abandoned businesses to explore. Old hotels, motels, gas stations, ghost towns, those kinds of places. If there was a house along with the business, then he checked it out, too.

A memory of one of his earlier solo explorations

came back to him. The place could have been the set created for the movie *Psycho;* they were so similar — the motel close to the road and the house on the hill behind it. Where was that place? For the life of him, he couldn't remember.

Mitch almost didn't go to the Kembleford Manor Hotel. When he saw the location in his online search, the distance from home to it almost put him off. Twelve hours of driving total. It didn't leave much time for sleeping or exploring. But, something in the description he'd found intrigued him. And it had nothing to do with the things Nicole saw, drew, or photographed.

He pulled into the drive-thru at a fast-food restaurant, ordered burgers, fries and a drink and drove home.

Nicole. Maybe that's what changed between him and Cooper. Him being protective of his younger sister. As she got older, she became more attractive. Mitch could see himself dating her. He enjoyed being in her company yesterday, even if she did get weird over things. Time would tell if anything would happen between them.

The photos and sketches proved that strange phenomena occurred at Kembleford Manor — in the mansion and out on the grounds.

Nicole grabbed the next box. This one at least had items that made sense to her despite not having seen them for ages. Baby books for her and her brothers. She picked up the top one and leafed through the pages. This one was Connor's. He should have it. She lifted the one her mother started for her next, and set it aside. That was something to look at later. Right now, the rest of the contents of this banker's box were more important. Still, that didn't stop her from taking a quick run-through of the book created for Cooper. It was practically identical to Connor's, but then they were identical twins, so it made sense in a strange way.

Beneath the baby books lay a folded and yellowed newspaper page. Nicole lifted it out and unfolded it. It was a copy of the *Pike Falls Courier*. Why did her mother have it? The headline on the front page stood out like a beacon.

PIKE FALLS COURIER

| Vol. 1431 | Tuesday, August 4, 1914 | Two cents |

ALBERT KEMBLEFORD DEAD OF SELF-INFLICTED GUNSHOT WOUND

John L. Smith, Staff Reporter

Police investigating fraud at the Kembleford Lumber Mill were called to the nearby home of its founder, Albert Kembleford, shortly after noon on July 31, 1914.

Discrepancies were noted in the lumber company's accounts during the annual audit. Further investigation led to the local Bailiff and constabulary being brought in. At the time of their arrival, Mr. Kembleford was not on the premises. Only his accounts clerk, son-in-law Bartholomew Randall, was onsite in the administrative area.

Before they could arrest him as an accessory after the fact, Mr. Randall bolted from the offices of the once-thriving enterprise. Police were then summoned to the deceased's home, Kembleford Manor, where Mr. Kembleford was found in his study, having held a Smith & Wesson Model 2 to his temple and pulled the trigger.

The situation so distressed Mr. Kembleford's daughter, Ophelia (wife of Bartholomew Randall), that the pregnant woman went into premature labour.

Mr. Randall, meanwhile, was arrested at the Kembleford home for his part in the embezzlement for trying to cover the issue by cooking the books.

Wow. Reporters sure didn't mince words in the newspapers of the day. Nicole was surprised they didn't mention blood spatter and brain and bone fragments splattered on the wall. The article tied in with the visions she'd seen when they explored there.

The death certificate. She'd photographed it. It was for Bartholomew and Ophelia's stillborn daughter. She returned to her laptop and clicked through the images until she found it. Despite enlarging it, the quality of the original was in such terrible shape that she couldn't do anything with it. At least not when she was only previewing the pictures. Possibly, if she were using her photo editing software. Nicole checked the image on her phone, and it was the same poor quality.

Another yellowed newspaper page came out of the box next. It was dated a week after the first one she hauled out that reported the death of Albert Kembleford.

PIKE FALLS COURIER

Vol. 1432   Tuesday, August 11, 1914   Two cents

A SECOND TRAGEDY AT KEMBLEFORD MANOR ON THE SAME DAY

John L. Smith, Staff Reporter

As reported in last week's edition of the Pike Falls Courier, Ophelia Kembleford, daughter of suicide victim Albert Kembleford, went into premature labour. Since that time, we have discovered the child, a girl, was stillborn. The infant barely weighed three pounds and was approximately three months early.

Ophelia Kembleford was the wife of Bartholomew Randall, the accounts clerk at the Kembleford Lumber Mill. He was arrested on the day of the two tragedies and is in jail awaiting a court date.

With the baby's father in jail and the grandfather also deceased, only Ophelia, her mother (Patience), her brother (James), and her sister (Lavinia) attended the funeral. The infant was buried in Union Cemetery, Pike Falls, on August 4, 1914, one day after the funeral and burial of Albert Kembleford in the same cemetery.

It leads one to wonder if the family or home is cursed.

That family was jinxed. That was the only thing Nicole could think of. Two deaths in one day. What else could it be?

She remembered the vision she had in the tower at the manor house. She didn't sketch Ophelia's suicide. Nor did she know when the young woman hanged herself. If the paper printed an article about it, it could be in one of these boxes.

Nicole returned her attention to this latest newspaper article and re-read it. That name. Patience. She was Albert Kembleford's wife. It should have occurred to her sooner. But it still didn't explain why her mother had these things. With any luck, she would come across more letters from Patience's mother. The twenty-year gap between letters made no sense — unless Patience destroyed them. What reason could she have had for doing such a thing?

The remaining contents of this box were babies' hair brushes, three pairs of knitted booties, three bonnets, and three sweaters. Two blue, one pink. By their small size, they had to be the first sweater sets her mother received for Nicole and her brothers. Maybe they were hand-knit by one of her grandmothers.

Nicole set the two newspaper clippings aside with the baby books, returned the rest of the contents to the box, put the lid back on it, and moved on to the next one.

The box Nicole selected next was a shoebox. There couldn't be much material in it. Another yellowed newspaper clipping. Why weren't they all kept together? She unfolded it. She might have given the ghost of Ophelia Kembleford Randall some privacy, but the newspaper certainly ate up the suicide. So far, all three Kembleford deaths had been reported on the front page. They were a prominent family in the town, so it made sense, but for the survivors, it seemed cruel.

PIKE FALLS COURIER

Vol. 1501	Tuesday, January 4, 1915	Two cents

THE KEMBLEFORD CURSE HAS TAKEN YET ANOTHER LIFE

John L. Smith, Staff Reporter

On the last day of 1914, December 31, Ophelia Kembleford, wife of Bartholomew Randall, daughter of the late Albert Kembleford and his wife, Patience, was found in the tower of the family home. She left no note, but it is assumed death was due to grief. First for the loss of her stillborn child, second for the self-inflicted death of her father, and third for the incarceration of her husband.

When found, her lifeless body was strung up by the neck in the Kembleford Manor tower. It is unknown how long she dangled there before being found by her sister, Lavinia. This cruel twist of fate happened on the youngest member of the family's birthday. Lavinia Kembleford was born on December 31, 1893.

The funeral for Mrs. Randall will be held tomorrow, and burial will follow in the spring.

The Kembleford Curse was aptly named. Three family deaths in one year. And poor Lavinia, made the gruesome discovery on her birthday. What would that do to a person's mental health? This clipping joined the others that she was taking to her brothers.

The Barnsley's Bakery logo. She should be working on it and not going through all these boxes of stuff that would likely end up going in the trash. So far, except for the baby items, nothing related to their family. It made no sense why these other things had been preserved and passed down.

A pair of white satin gloves wrapped in tissue paper. Dull grey was a more apt description of the colour, but they were once white. Who wore these back in the day? They looked like they were from the Victorian era. Perhaps Patience wore them to their children's christenings. There she went again. Trying to connect something that wasn't.

Beneath that were some old photographs which had been mounted on card stock embossed with patterns to look like a mat. The one on top was a man and woman with three children — one boy and two girls. The man looked like the one in the newspaper clipping. Was this Albert and Patience Kembleford and their family? The familiar yet younger face of Ophelia was recognizable. So the other little girl must be Lavinia. But who was the boy? He was mentioned in the newspaper article covering the stillbirth on the same day as Albert Kembleford's death. She grabbed the yellowed sheet of newsprint one more time. The boy's name was James. He was the oldest and left Kembleford Manor and Pike Falls before the deaths started happening and returned for the funerals.

Nicole thought about the packet of letters. One from James to his mother, Patience, was in the bundle. She would have to show these letters to her brothers or at least confess to taking them out of the house. They wouldn't be happy. Cooper especially. She'd take her lumps as and when. Now that the boy's identity in the family photograph was known, she continued perusing the other photos. Studio images of the three children. She squinted to read the date and photographer's name. Maybe it was time to take a break. She'd been at it all day since returning from Connor and Cooper's apartment.

Except when she sat in front of her computer at the table, Nicole had sat on the floor the rest of the day. She could barely move when she pried herself up from the hardwood surface, but at least her leg and foot weren't asleep like earlier.

Connor opened the fridge door and stared at the contents. Nothing appealed to him, yet it was his turn to make supper, so he had to come up with something. He checked the freezer next. A frozen lasagna was buried under a freezer burnt something. After more rooting around, he found a loaf of crusty bread that didn't look too bad. Supper sorted. He was sure there was a tub of garlic spread in the fridge so they could split the loaf in two, slather it with the stuff and warm it up, either in the oven with the main course or in the microwave.

"Lasagna and garlic bread," he yelled from the kitchen.

"Sounds good to me."

Oven preheating, two craft beers opened, Connor walked into the living room, and handed a can to his brother.

Cooper held the TV remote and flipped through the channels. He stopped at a movie that was just starting. One that they both liked and with the apartment's layout, they could watch it while they ate supper.

"I didn't know *Guns of Navarone* was on today," Connor said.

"Me neither. Not until just now." Cooper put the remote down and took a slug of beer.

The oven beeped, indicating it was up to temperature, so Connor slipped out, put in the lasagna, and set the timer for the cooking time. When that was done, he rejoined his brother. The bread could wait a while. It would go into the microwave if it wasn't thawed enough by the time they were ready to eat. They could spread the garlic butter on it at the table. It wouldn't be the first time.

"Wonder what Nicki's found on the SD card?" Cooper asked.

"Don't know. I hope she got some good shots, though. I think she took a photo for every sketch she made, and she drew a lot of pictures. It will probably take her a lifetime to go through and compare them all.

Whether Nicole took them to the apartment later or waited until Monday when she returned to work, she didn't know. Maybe she wouldn't take them until she had something to tie them into their family. There were still more boxes to go through. She had just scratched the surface. There were still boxes stacked in the hallway she hadn't touched yet.

If she could get through a box a night after work, she might get through them by the end of the following weekend. Unless they were out exploring some abandoned property, she'd have all day Saturday and Sunday to peruse the contents. Sure, she had laundry and housework to do, but her apartment was small, so it didn't take long.

Her stomach growled. She hadn't eaten since she ate a banana in the morning. She hauled herself from the floor and headed to the kitchen for something to eat. While the cupboards and fridge didn't have much in them, at least they hadn't reached Mother Hubbard's status yet. Nicole decided on tomato soup, made with milk, and a grilled cheese sandwich.

Chapter Thirty-One

OCTOBER 24, 2022

It was almost eleven o'clock, but Nicole was on the last box. Most of the others held nothing of any significant interest. Well, they did, but nothing that had anything to do with Kembleford Manor or the family.

At least this one showed some promise. No lurid headlines on newspaper clippings, but Nicole found a diary that had belonged to Lavinia Kembleford. Did she sit up and read it tonight? Or leave it for another time. The line in Patience's mother's letter saying that the girl could end up causing a scandal by becoming an unwed mother due to her flirtatious nature sprang into her mind and the decision was made.

Nicole took the diary to her room and placed it on her bedside table. She then went through her ritual of turning off lights and electronics, plugged her phone in to charge overnight, and got changed into her flannel pyjamas, then went back to the kitchen for a glass of water from the Brita jug in the fridge.

Sitting with her back against the headboard, Nicole picked up the diary and began to read.

Jan 1, 1910
Dear Diary,
I received you as a Christmas gift, so what better way to start the New Year. I'm so upset. I love a man, but he doesn't know I exist. I've tried many things to get him

to notice me but to no avail. He only has eyes for my older sister, Ophelia. Even on my birthday, yesterday. He paid little attention to me. Now, he did wish me a happy birthday, but that was all. I tried to get him to kiss me under the mistletoe because that's what you do. But he wanted no part of that.

Ophelia treats him abominably. If I were the one he was smitten with, I wouldn't treat him that way. This is the year I plan on doing something about it. I'm going to woo Bartholomew Randall away from her.

That entry was interesting. Nicole skimmed through the following entries. No mention of stealing her sister's boyfriend. The next one that his name appeared in was Valentine's Day.

February 14, 1910

Dear Diary,

I'm so angry. Sad, too. Bartholomew asked Father's permission to marry Ophelia. When Father granted it, he then proposed to her at dinner. What am I going to do?

At least today, she was more congenial to him. Still, it's not as lovely as I would be. I can't let them get married. Bartholomew should be mine. But how do I break them apart? And how do I get him to notice me? I'd have to throw myself at him, and I don't know if that would work; he's so in love with my sister.

Hmm ... curiouser and curiouser. What would Lavinia's next move be in her quest to steal Bartholomew from Ophelia? Nicole didn't figure the girl had a snowball's chance, but whatever she did, if she recorded it here in her diary, it would make titillating reading material. Lavinia was a determined sort of girl.

June 10, 1910

Dear Diary,

Ophelia and Bartholomew have set the date for their wedding. It will be a year today. I've tried everything possible to drive a wedge between them, but it didn't work. I have to admit defeat and set my sights on someone else.

That was a disappointment. Nicole was confident there would be fireworks or something spectacular. Lavinia didn't seem to be the sort to give up so easily. Unless some other poor, unsuspecting male had caught her eye.

Nicole skimmed through the rest of the entries. Nothing interesting. Mostly talk of the weather, the village gossip, being sick of hearing about her sister's wedding plans. And then the New Year's Eve entry.

December 31, 1910

Dear Diary,

Today was my birthday. Not one member of the family wished me a happy birthday. Not Mother. Not Father. Not even my brother and sister. And well, Bartholomew, you can forget about him. He's not even speaking to me. I don't know why he's so angry with me. It's not like I told him an untruth. I plainly told him that I was in love with him and could make him far more happy than Ophelia ever could. So now, no one cares that today is my birthday. It didn't help that I said it at the breakfast table. Bartholomew takes most of his meals with us now that he and Ophelia are engaged. Well, when I said that, there were gasps of horror from everyone at the table. Even the maid, Matilda. She almost dropped the tray of breakfast things she carried. This was the worst birthday of my life.

The poor girl put her foot in it well. Both feet. Nicole pitied her despite never having met her or knowing what she was like as a person. Were there more of Lavinia's diaries in the boxes? Or did she only keep one for the year 1910?

It was late, but by now, Nicole was wide awake. Sleep was impossible now, so she threw the blankets off and returned to the living room, where she sat on the couch next to the box where she had found the diary. There were more photographs of the family. Some appeared to have been taken in a studio, while others outside but still bore the photographer's stamp in the lower right corner. There was a picture of the boathouse. Back then, it was pristine. Not old and decrepit as she knew it. It even boasted a cupola on the roof with a weather vane on its peak.

Stuck down the side of the box, an empty paper towel roll was wedged into the corner. Nicole picked it out and discovered it wasn't just the cardboard tube. There was something inside it. She worked away at the papers inside using her index and middle fingers.

When she finally got it out, she unrolled it. A chart. Her name was on it. It was one of those. The graphic type escaped her, but it started with her and worked back through her parents, their parents, their grandparents, and even more generations. And then she saw it. Her maternal great-grandmother. She couldn't wait to show her brothers. But she didn't think they would be receptive to a visit at three in the morning. Rather than put the document back in its packaging, she placed it on top of the other things she was taking to show her brothers when she went to work.

After her discovery in the wee hours of the morning, Nicole couldn't wait to share the news with her brothers. With the required documents, newspaper clippings, and photos boxed up, she was ready to head into the office. The last thing she did was put her laptop, with her camera's SD card still in the slot, and work sketchbook on top of the vital papers.

Traffic that morning was horrendous. Maybe it was because she was anxious and excited, or perhaps that had nothing to do with it, and the morning commute from her apartment to the strip mall was always a nightmare.

When she finally arrived, Nicole parked behind their office and carried the box through the rear door. An opened stack of wide-carriage fanfold computer paper marked up with highlighters sat on the table.

That wasn't a good sign. It meant her brothers were conducting a major debug of the website they were building for their client. "Connor, Cooper, you have to come see what I found out," she called as she swept the paperwork aside with the carton.

"Hey! Watch what you're doing," Cooper shouted. "There's a lot of work there. Don't mess it up."

"Keep your hair on, brother, dear."

"What's up, sis?" Connor asked as he strode to the table where his siblings stood.

Nicole took the lid off the box and removed her work-related gear. "Remember when we discussed exploring Kembleford Manor, and I said the name sounded familiar?"

"Yeah. And I told you it was from you watching *Father Brown* all the time," said Connor.

"That has nothing to do with it. After Mummy's cancer came back, she got into genealogy."

"I didn't know that. Did you Coop?"

"Before I go any further, I need to confess to something. When we were in the tower room, I found a packet of letters in the trunk. I didn't put them back. I brought them home."

"How could you, Nicki? That's theft. We never take anything from the places we explore," Cooper said.

"I know, but in a strange way, they belong to us, too. Turns out Mummy's a descendant of the Kembleford family that owned the mansion and the lumber mill in Pike Falls."

"No way," said Connor.

Nicole dug out the family tree document. "Right here." She pointed to the chart. "Mummy's grandmother was Sheila Kembleford, and *her* grandfather was Albert Kembleford, who started the mill. But wait." She opened her personal sketchbook to the drawings she did the day they explored the mansion and flipped to the page where she'd sketched her encounter on the stairs. "The man — ghost — I saw on the stairs was Albert."

"How can you tell? I mean, this is his back," said Cooper.

She flipped to the next page. "This is an image I'll

never get out of my head." The image of the same encounter was on the page but from the opposite angle. Although the face wasn't severely damaged, a large, jagged hole removed a piece from the side of his head. At least the sketch didn't show the gore from the bullet wound. "Kembleford Manor isn't evil; it's shrouded in tragedy and sadness."

"This is wild. Who would have expected that we'd end up exploring a piece of our own history," said Cooper.

Also by Melanie Robertson-King

The Consequences Collection
Tim's Magic Christmas
The Secret of Hillcrest House
A Shadow in the Past (second edition)
Shadows From Her Past
YESTERDAY TODAY ALWAYS
Cole's Notes (Revised version)
It Happened on Dufferin Terrace
It Happened in Gastown
It Happened at Percé Rock
It Happened at Lake Louise
All Aboard the Canadian with Buddy and his Four
Fantastic Furry Friends!
(King Park Press)

Cole's Notes (A Short Story)
*EFD1: Starship Goodwords – a cross genre
anthology*
(CARRICK PUBLISHING, 2012)

Future Titles in the *It Happened* Series ...
featuring the Layne and Scott families

It Happened in Niagara Falls

MELANIE ROBERTSON-KING

https://melanierobertson-king.com

Melanie Robertson-King has always been a fan of the written word. Growing up as an only child, her face was almost always buried in a book from the time she could read. Her father was one of the thousands of Home Children sent to Canada through the auspices of The Orphan Homes of Scotland, and she has been fortunate to be able to visit her father's homeland many times and even met the Princess Royal (Princess Anne) at the orphanage where he was raised.